A Terrible Tide

A TERRIBLE TIDE

A Story of the Newfoundland Tsunami of 1929

SUZANNE MEADE

Second Story Press

Library and Archives Canada Cataloguing in Publication

Title: A terrible tide : a story of the Newfoundland tsunami of 1929 /
 Suzanne Meade.
Names: Meade, Suzanne, 1973- author.
Identifiers: Canadiana (print) 2021013562X | Canadiana (ebook)
 20210135816 | ISBN 9781772602111 (softcover) | ISBN
 9781772602128 (EPUB)
Classification: LCC PS8626.E2325 T47 2021 | DDC jC813/.6—dc23

Cover © Hayden Maynard/www.i2iart.com

Edited by Kathryn White
Designed by Melissa Kaita

All photos courtesy of the Marina Pelley Collection, Archives and Special
Collections, Queen Elizabeth II Library, Memorial University

Printed and bound in Canada

*Second Story Press gratefully acknowledges the support of the Ontario Arts
Council and the Canada Council for the Arts for our publishing program.
We acknowledge the financial support of the Government of Canada through
the Canada Book Fund.*

Published by
SECOND STORY PRESS
20 Maud Street, Suite 401
Toronto, ON M5V 2M5
www.secondstorypress.ca

A TERRIBLE TIDE

A Story of the Newfoundland Tsunami of 1929

SUZANNE MEADE

Second Story Press

Library and Archives Canada Cataloguing in Publication

Title: A terrible tide : a story of the Newfoundland tsunami of 1929 /
   Suzanne Meade.
Names: Meade, Suzanne, 1973- author.
Identifiers: Canadiana (print) 2021013562X | Canadiana (ebook)
   20210135816 | ISBN 9781772602111 (softcover) | ISBN
   9781772602128 (EPUB)
Classification: LCC PS8626.E2325 T47 2021 | DDC jC813/.6—dc23

Cover © Hayden Maynard/www.i2iart.com

Edited by Kathryn White
Designed by Melissa Kaita

All photos courtesy of the Marina Pelley Collection, Archives and Special
Collections, Queen Elizabeth II Library, Memorial University

Printed and bound in Canada

*Second Story Press gratefully acknowledges the support of the Ontario Arts
Council and the Canada Council for the Arts for our publishing program.
We acknowledge the financial support of the Government of Canada through
the Canada Book Fund.*

ONTARIO ARTS COUNCIL
CONSEIL DES ARTS DE L'ONTARIO

Canada Council   Conseil des Arts
for the Arts   du Canada

Funded by the Government of Canada
Financé par le gouvernement du Canada

Canadä

Published by
SECOND STORY PRESS
20 Maud Street, Suite 401
Toronto, ON M5V 2M5
www.secondstorypress.ca

MIX
Paper from
responsible sources
FSC
FSC® C103567

CONTENTS

*For Nana, who inspired me
to write about Newfoundland.*

Chapter 1

AN INTERRUPTED CELEBRATION

Burin Peninsula, Newfoundland
Monday, November 18, 1929, 5:00 p.m.

"C'mon, birthday girl," my sister Winnie said as she limped past me on her uneven legs. Opening the cupboard, she looked over at Mom. "Can we use the fancy dishes? Please?"

I scowled at her. "But it's my birthday! Why do I have to set the table?"

"Celia Rose," Mom said, in her very serious voice. She frowned for a moment at Winnie, then gave a small shrug. "All right then. You just be extra careful."

I grinned at Winnie, secretly pleased to use the new dishes Dad had ordered special from London as a gift for Mom after a good fishing season last year. I carefully lifted the plates from the shelf and carried them to the table. They were heavy, made of porcelain, and painted with gold scrolls and fanciful birds. Peacocks maybe, or was it pheasants? Beautiful birds, whichever they were.

Winnie grabbed a handful of cutlery and began to lay out seven places. Everyone was home tonight, even my older sister Viola. She didn't get much time off from her job in Lamaline. The larger village was only a few miles away, but it felt further.

I had just set down the last dish when the floor began to vibrate. Winnie squeaked in surprise, dropping the knives and forks. They clattered to the table as the vibrations grew stronger. The voices from the sitting room—where Dad, Viola, and the boys had gathered— fell silent. I lurched toward Mom, who stood frozen by the stove. Her eyes were wide, her mouth scrunched as if she'd been about to say something but had thought better of it.

"What—?" I began.

Viola shrieked as the shaking intensified. Plates rattled and the cast-iron pots on the stove danced a strange little jig. The windows shook as if there was a norther blowing, white curtains billowing. Great-Nan's portrait,

2

in its place of honor on the wall by the window, bounced against the whitewashed boards and tilted squish-ways. Ominous creaking came from every direction.

"What in the blazes?" Henry exclaimed from the other room, mirroring my own thoughts.

I giggled nervously, then stepped toward Winnie. She lost her balance and landed hard, crying out in pain. The cupboard door swung open, and the everyday plates slid out, falling to the floor in a smash of crockery. I gasped. Dad appeared in the sitting room doorway.

"Outside," he said sharply.

Viola and my brothers followed him into the kitchen. Henry was near hopping in excitement. Eddie pushed past me and scooped Winnie up in his arms. Six months ago, he wouldn't have been able to lift her like that. He'd grown some inches and filled out working on the boat with Dad and Uncle Bert since he'd decided that he'd had enough of school.

We scrambled to pull on our coats before heading into the cold evening air. Eddie carried Winnie out and set her carefully on her feet once they were on flat planks. I handed over her coat. Everything outside swayed too. The fish room at the far end of the dock teetered but did not fall. The masts of all the boats tipped back and forth, moving far more quickly than they would on normal waves.

From all around came a babble of frightened voices as neighbors came spilling out of their houses. Men, women, and children gathered on the swaying pier. By the crowd, it seemed as if the whole village was there— some eighty or so people, all chattering at once. There were panicked shrieks, moans, and muttered prayers. Some voices rose above the others, arguing. People looked in every direction, searching for the source of the upheaval.

My own family was arguing loudly about the tremors.

"It can't have been an airplane, Dad," Viola protested. "They don't make the ground shake like that."

Dad's mouth was set in a stubborn line. "Coulda been, young miss. I hear they make a terrible noise when they fly low overhead."

Viola shook her head and opened her mouth to answer.

"Why would there be an airplane here?" I asked, peering up at the sky. I didn't expect to see anything, but I couldn't help looking anyway.

"I think it was an explosion," Henry said, turning this way and that. "Over by the wharf, maybe? The stored coal, I expect."

"We'd see that from here," Eddie replied, looking toward the wooden warehouse at the government dock.

"Smoke or fire, maybe both."

"Explosion's shorter anyway," Dad said. "Shaking's been going on for some few minutes now."

"Could be more than one explosion," Viola said, tapping her chin. "Like in Halifax, with the ships."

I didn't know of any ships nearby with munitions and started to say so, but no one was listening. Henry and Eddie talked over everyone, words muddling together. While they argued, the tremors lessened and then stopped. I glanced at Winnie, who was now perched on a crate.

"What do you think happened?" I asked, sitting beside her.

"I don't know," she replied in a small, frightened voice. Her back was hunched, and I could feel her trembling. "I didn't like it, CeeCee."

I put my arm across her shoulders and squeezed gently. "Me either. But it seems to be stopping now." We sat quietly for a moment as the excited babble around us calmed. Mom and Henry moved closer.

I had a silly, ridiculous thought. Before I could stop myself, I blurted, "Maybe a giant farted." I flushed as soon as I said it, but maybe it would make her laugh.

Henry, naturally, giggled. Even Winnie grinned at me. But Mom sighed. "Girls who want to be ladies don't talk like that," she said sternly.

"I'm not a lady," I protested.

"You're thirteen now," Mom replied. "Near grown and a big help to me."

I scowled at her. "Still not a lady."

"No," Mom said, giving me another of her serious looks. "I guess you're not."

What did she mean by that? Was she really serious, or was she twiting me? I frowned, trying to puzzle it out.

Another thought popped into my head. "Where's Boomer?"

"Out and about, as usual," Viola said, wrinkling her nose. She'd never been a big fan of letting the dog in the house.

"He must be scared," I protested, "thinking the world's gone some crazy." I pictured his big brown eyes, set wide above his heavy muzzle. If he was here, he'd look mournfully at me, and I'd scritch his ears to make him feel better.

"It's a dog, Celia. He'll be fine," Viola grumbled.

"How can you know that, Vi? He's got feelings. He thinks things. Have you seen him when he wants attention or food? Just because he can't talk…." I glared at Viola. How could she be so uncaring?

She flipped her bobbed hair and gave a dramatic sigh. "He'll come trundling home when he's ready, smelling of fish and wet dog. You can count on it. He's probably swimming up at the pond right now. You know how he loves the water."

"But—" I began.

"That's enough, Celia," Mom said firmly. I knew it was the end of the discussion. I'd have to go looking for him later, then.

Night settled on the village, and the air grew colder. Winnie and I huddled together for warmth, listening to the continued chatter of everyone around us.

"Do you think the shaking will come back?" Winnie asked, fumbling for my hand.

I squeezed her fingers gently through our mittens. "I don't know. I sure hope not."

She laid her head on my shoulder. "I want to go home."

"Well, let's see what the others think. Maybe it'll be safe enough."

Mom and Nan hurried over as I rose to my feet. "George and Bert have checked the house," Mom said, looking from me to Winnie. "They say things seem sound. Let's get you kids warmed up."

"Are you sure?" I said, worry settling into my stomach. I couldn't forget the feeling of the world shaking under me. How could the house possibly be safe after all that?

"As sure as we can be, child," Nan said briskly. "Now come along."

Winnie pushed herself upright and took hold of my hand again. Her mouth turned down in a worried frown.

"Henry!" Mom called, beckoning to the group of boys gathered at the edge of the dock.

My brother looked over at us. He didn't look too happy at being called away. Ollie Taylor yelled something to him, but Henry just shook his head and followed us into the house. Nan poked her head in and then continued on to her place.

Inside, there were only a few signs of disturbance. Aside from the smashed crockery, one of the fancy plates had fallen to the floor and broken clean in half. A pair of forks lay neatly across the broken porcelain. Everything else was in its place.

Viola bent down and picked up the dishes. She laid the fancy one carefully on the table, then carried the broken bits of the everyday plates over to the wash basin.

Mom, meanwhile, peered into the pot left on the

stove and grimaced. "Well, that's that," she said, scraping the burnt potatoes into the scrap bin.

Winnie plunked down on a chair, still wearing her coat. I couldn't blame her. My nerves jangled, and every second I expected the house to come tumbling down around us. I sat beside her and leaned my elbows on the table. Henry hovered in the doorway.

"I'm hungry," he said.

I was too, but I didn't want to eat. The thought of putting food in my stomach made me want to hurl.

"We've some biscuits," Mom said. "Not likely to have much else for a bit."

Henry scrunched up his face and stuck out his tongue.

"I could maybe have a biscuit," Winnie said.

Viola fetched the basket and a pot of butter. Everyone but me dug in, spreading the soft, creamy butter on the day-old biscuits. Normally I'd have been right there, but not tonight.

Just then, Eddie burst through the door. "Uncle Ray's on the telephone down at the store," he said, waving his hands excitedly. "It's amazing! Talking to him clear from Burin. Why, it's just like he's standing beside you. You'd never believe they're forty miles away. C'mon, they're waiting to talk to us."

My heart fluttered. I wasn't sure if it was excitement

at the thought of talking on the telephone or my nerves. Even Mom and Viola had perked up at the news.

"I can't believe it's that clear," Mom said, shrugging into her coat.

"I didn't either till I heard him," Eddie said. "I never heard anything like it my whole life."

"What did they say?" Viola demanded. "Have they had the shaking over in Burin too?"

"Dad's talking to him now," Eddie replied. "I didn't have much chance."

"Meet you there," I said over my shoulder as I headed outside. I couldn't wait to talk to Uncle Ray. We hadn't seen him since last summer when he'd stopped by on the boat while fishing. It had been even longer since we'd seen our cousins. Whatever did one say on the telephone though? *Hello, how are you?* seemed far too everyday for such a big moment.

My booted feet rattled the boards of the dock as I ran past the flakes piled with the last of the drying cod. Taylor's General Store was on the far side of the big wharf where the coastal boats pulled in. Dark figures crossed back and forth between the shop window and the kerosene lamp, creating flickering shadows. I hesitated. Would I even get a chance to use the telephone? It seemed like a day for adults to talk, not kids. Not even on my birthday.

I was still standing there in the shadows when Henry and Viola appeared.

"Something wrong?" Viola said, her eyes flicking from me to the figures inside.

"No," I replied, scuffing my toes on the boards. "I just thought it'd be more fair if we all went in together after all."

Henry exhaled in a quick puff. "I didn't think you were waiting."

"Changed my mind."

"Well let's go in. It's freezing out here," Viola said as she opened the door. There wasn't much to do but follow her. We pushed past our chattering neighbors, still arguing about the source of the tremors.

Dad stood close by the counter with the telephone receiver against his ear. When I came to stand beside him, he grinned lopsidedly and held up one hand. "Yes, that's what we were thinking," he said, speaking into the mouthpiece. It looked like a metal flower mounted on top of a brass candlestick. "Some said an explosion, but that's not likely if you've had shaking down your way." He paused, nodding at something he heard through the telephone. "From underground? Could be, b'y. Could be. You've not heard anything from further out? No, telegraph's down here."

Henry grabbed my arm. "I want a turn!" he said, hopping up and down.

"Me too," I snapped. "Just wait for once, will you?" I examined the telephone while we waited. How in heaven's name did this funny-looking bit of machinery carry voices over such distances in no time at all?

Dad said good-bye and held out the receiver. Henry grabbed it before I could. "Hello?" he said, very loudly.

I sighed and leaned against the counter. When Eddie arrived with Mom and Winnie, he pushed his way through to the counter and grinned at me.

"He doesn't have to yell," Eddie said quietly, speaking right into my ear. "It's not like he has to make his voice heard the whole forty miles to Burin on his own."

I chuckled. "It's hard to believe, though."

"True," Eddie said. "You had a turn yet?"

"Nah, Henry grabbed quicker."

"Impatient little tallywack."

"He is that," I said.

Bessie Taylor walked along behind the counter. She had the right to be back there, unlike me, seeing as this was her grandfather's store. I glanced at her from the corner of my eye. Whatever did she want?

"We've had a handful of telephone calls already," said Bessie, leaning over the counter to make sure I could hear her clear among the chatter. "Is this the first for your family?"

I nodded. My mouth twisted into a frown. Leave it to Bessie to lord anything over me.

"Well," she said with a sly smile, "I'm sure you'll have others, someday."

"I'm sure," I replied, turning away to focus on Henry and his side of the conversation. He was chattering about some fish he'd caught jigging in the bay.

Dad reached over and tapped Henry on the shoulder. "Hey, b'y. Others be waiting." He firmly took the receiver and handed it to me.

Henry glared daggers at me as I held the conical device to my ear. Uncle Ray's voice was tinny but clear, saying Henry's name. I stepped closer and spoke into the mouthpiece. "Hello? It's Celia."

The telephone crackled in my ear, and I jerked my head away. My uncle said something, but I didn't hear him clearly. Before I could ask him about it, the floor began to vibrate. The air around me filled with shrieks of panic. Shelves swayed, dumping small items to the whitewashed wood below our feet. There was yelling on the other end of the line.

Dad grabbed the earpiece out of my hand. "Ray? Yes, it started up here again too. Sure. Telephone again later." He carefully placed the receiver back on the cradle. I watched the whole telephone tremble as the store shook.

There was a terrible babble of noise all around as people chattered and cried. One clear voice yelled, "'Tis the end of the world, I'm telling you!" I couldn't tell who it was. Eddie grabbed hold of one of my hands, Henry the other, and we ran for the door. Mom and Winnie met us outside, where there was a bustle of activity.

My hands were sore from holding so tight to my brothers. I let go, exhaling in relief, and looked over at Winnie. She tried to smile but only managed to look frightened.

People were scurrying around like crabs, making as much noise as a bunch of curlews fighting over fish guts on the beach. Winnie clung tight to my arm as we made our slow way along the dock and back toward the house. Mom and Viola walked just in front of us. I scanned the area, checking for any sign of Boomer.

Partway home, Uncle Bert caught up with us. "Can you come over to Mom's place please, Addie? She's taken a fall and split her scalp a fine bit. She'd appreciate you coming to have a look."

"Of course. Vi, get the kids home. I'm sure it'll be safer to be warm inside than sitting out here in the cold. I'll go deal with your Nan and be home in a trice."

Chapter 2
MYSTERY AT THE BAY

Monday, 7:15 p.m.

When Mom came back a short time later, the first thing she did was straighten the old photograph of Great-Nan on the wall. Then she turned and gave us a tired smile.

"How's Nan?" Viola asked.

Mom laughed. "Oh, you know that old woman. She never loses her head. I think she'd be barking orders and running roughshod over everyone regardless of what happened." She sank into a chair. "The cut on her head's not deep. I got her bandaged up and bound it tight. We'll check it tomorrow in the light."

"Any word about the *Maggie Grace*?" Winnie said.

"Nothing yet, m'girl. I did hear the menfolk talking—like a bunch of curlews, they were. Chattering in the laneways. No one seemed too worried about the boats, though."

"We still haven't seen Boomer," I said, struggling to stay calm while my palms sweated and my mind raced. "He must be right scared, now that the whole world's been shaking twice."

Viola sniffed haughtily, but Mom put a stop to that with a look. "I'm sure he's fine, Celia. We can send Eddie to have a look-see when he gets back, though. Just to be sure."

"I could go," I said eagerly. "He and Dad are busy. Could be a while yet. Right?"

Mom shook her head and gave a tired sigh. "Best not. It's dark, and who knows if there'll be more of that shaking. Vi's got one thing right—Boomer can look after himself. He's a big, strong dog and used to working. We'll get it sorted when the men come home."

"But—"

"I said no, Celia. Stay safe here and wait."

"Fine! I thought he was our family dog, but clearly no one cares about him except for me."

With an exasperated huff, I stomped up the stairs to the narrow room I shared with Winnie and flopped onto the bed. The patchwork quilt was soft under my knees. I traced the stitching with one finger, thinking of Mom and Nan piecing this quilt together. How long ago had it been now? Five years or so, if memory served me.

I rolled over and stared up at the ceiling. How could they be so heartless? Boomer had to be scared, wherever he was. What if he was hurt? What if he was trapped? There were dips and holes all around—he could have fallen in or had rocks fall on top of him. What if he couldn't get home for some reason—any reason at all? They all seemed so sure, but I wasn't.

I sat up and wandered over to the window. The itch to move was too strong for me to stay lying abed. Outside, the moon had risen, drowning out the stars and laying a clear, bright path across the water. Soft light glowed from the fallen snow. I looked out over the bay. It wasn't that dark out, not really. And wasn't I nearly grown, as Mom had said? Thirteen wasn't a child, after all. Eddie was only two years older, and Mom called him one of the men. No reason I needed to wait for him and Dad. I hesitated. Mom likely wouldn't agree with me. No need for her to know, though, was there?

I knew what I had to do. Boomer needed me, and so I would find him. Mom would understand, once we both got home safe.

Plan set firm in my mind, I headed back downstairs. It took real focus to walk normally. I wanted to tiptoe but that was a sure giveaway that something was up. Mom had settled by the lamp in the kitchen with her darning basket. She glanced up at me and raised an eyebrow. Her expression made it clear that she wasn't happy. Was she upset with me over the dog? Or was she just worried about the craziness of the evening?

"Just taking care of business," I said, hoping my voice didn't sound too strained. I paused for a moment, then shoved my feet into my boots, grabbed my coat, and settled the navy wool around my body. It was cold enough—surely she wouldn't find it odd for me to dress for the chill just to go to the outhouse.

Outside, the frigid air took my breath away. I closed the door firmly behind me so as not to let the cold in and picked my way along the path to our small outdoor toilet. The moon cast plenty of light to see by. I didn't really need to go, but Mom could likely hear the screech of the hinges from inside. Best to at least pretend. I opened the door, then closed it again a moment later. Satisfied that my plan was working, I began to sneak in earnest—away from the house at last.

Shadowy figures moved along the paths and tracks between the houses, and agitated voices called out. Mostly deep voices, but here and there a higher-pitched female voice punctuated the conversation. I tried to think where Boomer might be, where he would have gone if he was scared. Toward the bay, to the boat, where he was used to rocking and swaying at sea? Or inland, away from possible sources of danger? I turned one way and then the other, straining to catch some sign of Boomer's large, dark form against the snow. Nothing.

The boat, I decided. He'd go to the dock and get on a boat. If not the *Maggie Grace*, maybe someone else's. Even a dory would make him feel more at ease. They rocked on the waves same as the bigger skiffs, and he was out on the boat with Dad nearly every day during fishing season. I was sure he'd rather feel the boat rocking than the ground.

Our wooden dock was mostly clear of snow on account of the men walking down to the fish house. The moon cast wavering shadows all along the wooden planks. I peered this way and that, looking for Boomer's fuzzy head poking up. My attention elsewhere, I collided with a solid form and stumbled backward.

"Celia? That you, little sis?" Eddie reached out to steady me. I jumped guiltily, hoping he couldn't see my expression. I was sure my face showed clear as day that

I was doing something I shouldn't be. It certainly felt warm and flushed to me.

"What are you doing out and about?"

"Checking for Boomer," I said. "You didn't see him down by the *Maggie Grace*, did you?"

"No, I've not seen that old Newf. What's the worry?"

"He must be scared, what with all the shaking, don't you think?"

Eddie laughed. "That dog is the calmest creature I've ever met. Don't worry, I'm sure he's fine."

"He may be used to hauling things and even swimming long distances," I said. "But I've got to find him and make sure he's all right. For my sake."

"Does Mom know where you are?"

My heart jumped into my throat and threatened to strangle me. "Yes," I said, hoping my voice didn't sound too squeaky.

Eddie punched me gently on the shoulder. "Mind yourself and stay out of trouble, girl. I won't go running to Mom, but I'd wager she thinks you're somewhere else."

"Thanks, Eddie. I'll be careful."

I paused for a moment to breathe and let my heart slow its frantic pounding as Eddie loped off to rejoin the other young men. If Boomer wasn't at the *Maggie*

Grace, maybe he'd be hidden at the flakes. He'd surely find a cozy spot there, among the racks we used for drying cod. Someplace where he felt safe and could possibly snag himself a choice bit of fish. I resumed my search.

"Boomer!" I called softly into the darkness. Then several more times, louder. I peered around and under the wooden frames of the drying racks, the scent of pine needles sharp in my nose. The moon cast strange shadows in its wavering light, but there was no sign of Boomer's heavy muzzle poking up among the piled fish. I called out again and again, but he didn't appear. Maybe he'd gone inland after all. I stopped calling.

As I fell silent, a bizarre sound reached my ears—a loud, low sucking noise followed by a low-pitched rumble. The sound wrapped around me like a sudden fog. Mystified, I wandered to the small fish hut at the end of the dock. The strong, familiar scent of fish guts surrounded me. I peered out to sea. What in the name of hell? The water in the bay was draining away like some giant hole had sprung in the bottom of the ocean.

Over several minutes the boats, which had been tied up tight for the night, sank below the edge of the docks and stuck into the mud that piled up there. Further out in the bay, one large schooner tipped onto its side, sails dragging in the mud as the water disappeared. This was like no tide I'd ever seen. There was no sensible explanation for it.

I rubbed my eyes and looked again. Instead of the usual reflection off the water, the moonlight glimmered weakly from wet patches in the mud. It gave everything an eerie glow. Strange lumps and piles of debris made for an alien landscape. The low groaning continued. Maybe there really was a monster out there somewhere.

Indistinct voices rumbled nearby, nearly drowned out by the grumbling and sucking noise that surrounded me. I looked around. Over on the Irvine dock, a couple of men stood staring out at the bay, much as I'd been doing. I shrank back. Was one of them Dad? Then I wondered—had they seen Boomer? I had just decided to call out and ask when the noise changed. Louder. Deeper. I looked out as far as I could into the bay, but now there was no water at all. Was something drinking it all up?

Suddenly panicked voices yelled over the growing noise. "RUN! Run, the tide's rising fast! GO!"

My head snapped up, all my senses on high alert now. What was going on? Far out, at the end of the bay, was a rising crest of water. It foamed and frothed as it raced along the rocky shore. That was more than enough for me. I turned tail and ran as fast as my legs could carry me.

It was a flat race between me and the water. As I ran, I dodged several wooden crates and bounded over a neat coil of rope. My feet slipped on the wet boards, and I scrambled to stay upright. The rush of water behind me sounded like a monster, growling as it gave chase. No way was I going to let it catch me!

I was already wheezing in the cold when I passed our house in the darkness. I didn't see anyone, but the kitchen door caught my eye, banging open in the wind. Had they run already? For a heartbeat I slowed. Winnie. Was she safe somewhere ahead? There was no time to stop. I had to keep going. There were a few dark figures on the path in front of me. Who? I ran faster, the cold air working against me. My breathing felt heavy, my lungs sore. From every direction came frightened voices, yelling instructions or screaming in panic. The thin wail of a terrified baby.

I caught up to the people fleeing before me. My elderly neighbors, the Irvines. We exchanged a look but did not speak. The roar of the water was just too loud. Other people ran nearby, impossible to make out in the darkness. And there—the distinctive limping figure of Winnie. Mom, Viola, and Henry ran beside her. None of them had their coats. Viola had hold of Winnie's hand. Mom's head was swiveling back and forth. What was she looking for—me? And where were Dad and Eddie? Somewhere further ahead or somewhere behind, perhaps already in the water?

I glanced behind us. The gigantic wall of water was rushing ever closer. A boat rode the crest of the wave— one of the fishing schooners. It was headed right for us. I had to go faster. Panic spurred me on. Somehow, I gained speed as I rounded the path beside the freshwater pond. Inland and away was our only chance of escape. Behind me, someone screamed, and then the sound was cut off. I didn't want to think about what that meant.

I wasn't fast enough. Before I reached higher ground, out past the Taylor house, the wave came crashing down in a bitter cold torrent. I was swept off my feet by the rush of water. Wood splintered all around me as the boat slammed into the ground. Water swirled, pulling me in every direction. Bits of debris floated close by. I grabbed for something solid, trying to pull myself up to get a good breath. I couldn't see anything, but I could hear horrendous creaks and groans, along with the piercing sound of human voices howling and wailing. My lungs screamed for air. I inhaled, getting a mouthful of acrid ocean water. I choked and spluttered, thrashing around for something to hold on to.

Suddenly I felt myself lifted, pulled against the current by the collar of my coat. Something—some-one—had grabbed hold of me. My head rose above the water, and I took a great gasping breath. Salt spray stung my eyes, blurring my vision. It was hard not to struggle against the firm grip pulling me along. The water was bitter cold, and my legs and arms began to go numb.

Another rush of water pushed up behind me, shov-ing me forward. Was I about to smash into the shore or a house, like the schooner had? I imagined my body broken and bloody on the shore and began to panic again. My flailing hands connected with thick fur and strong muscles, and I realized abruptly who my savior was. Boomer! He must have been nearby after all.

Kicking for all I was worth and clinging to the dog's heavy fur coat, I propelled myself toward dry land. At least I hoped that was what I was doing. I was so turned around that I wasn't sure which way we were going any-more. Surely Boomer knew, though. He must. I wasn't ready to die tonight, just as I turned thirteen.

The helpful push of water behind me slowed, then stopped, and finally reversed. Suddenly we were swim-ming against the tide, fighting to maintain our position and not be swept out to sea. Exhaustion overtook me. Could I keep going much longer? Every kick became smaller and weaker, and the pull of the ocean grew stronger. Soon I would not be able to swim anymore. Soon, Boomer would grow too tired to help me. We were both going to drown, lost at sea with the flotsam and debris of our home.

In a brief moment of calm when the sea settled, Boomer and I bumped up against a solid piece of wood. Part of the wharf or of someone's house? I couldn't tell. Blind in the dark, I gripped the edge of the wood with cold-numbed fingers. I had to pull myself up. I couldn't swim any further, and I was going to sink. The thick wool coat that had kept me warm so far was now just added weight, hindering my ability to swim, but it was keeping me from freezing. Even wet, the heavy wool would trap heat from my body and that was what I needed right now. You didn't grow up here without knowing something about surviving.

My arm muscles screamed at me, pain shooting through them. I kicked my feet and pushed hard with my arms. Something bumped against me. When I turned, I saw it was a wooden platform. Bit by bit, I crawled up onto it. My waterlogged coat dragged at me, threatening to pull me backward. Sprawling across the width of the wood, I took a few deep breaths and began to shiver. Wet as I was, the air felt like ice. How long could a person survive like this?

I had a terrible thought and jolted upright. Where

was my dog? Had he abandoned me? Had he been swept away by the tide, too weak to go on? The moonlight reflecting off the water wasn't much help—there were too many shadows, strange shapes of bits and bobs floating nearby.

"Boomer!" I called, my voice hoarse from all the salt water. "Boomer, c'mere boy!"

There was a soft thump from behind me, followed by a familiar whuffing sound. There he was! Now, could he get up on the platform with me?

"C'mon, Boomer. Up—up with me!"

The dog's dark, furry head was near level with the edge of the boards. How could we get his paws up so that he could scramble aboard with me? And how could we make sure he didn't tip me back into the deep while he did it? I turned my body carefully, wriggling around so that I lay nose to nose with the dog. Reaching out, I stroked his sopping-wet fur with trembling fingers.

"We've got this, boy," I said softly. "You helped me, now it's my turn."

He was a big dog—heavier than me. I had to do something, though, or I was going to lose him. That thought was unbearable. Just grabbing that thick fur was not going to help. It would slip out of my numb hands and do nothing except pull on his skin. Could I get my arms under his front legs and lift him that way?

There was a risk of me tipping back into the bay, but I couldn't think of anything else. I inched forward, still stroking Boomer's wet fur. The platform tilted slightly toward him as I inched closer to the edge.

"Trust me, boy," I whispered, plunging my hands into the frigid water and slipping my arms under his wide chest. My makeshift raft tilted even further as I struggled to lift. From beneath the water, I felt the vibration as Boomer's heavy paws scrabbled against the wood. I tugged, pulling him toward me. His weight sent the edge of the platform well under the water, and I scuttled backward before he tipped me in. He chuffed at me, webbed paws scrambling, and managed to get himself fully up on the boards. We rocked, tipping back and forth as our raft settled. Boomer sat down next to me. His breath was warm on my face as he panted. It smelled strongly of fish.

"Good dog, Boomer. We did it!"

Shivering, I reached out to embrace him. He was wet too, but some heat radiated from his body. Maybe that would help me stay warm.

"Lie down, boy," I said, patting the weathered wood beside me. He lowered himself to his belly and reached out to sniff my face, then gently licked it. It tickled. I couldn't help but giggle in hysterical relief. I rolled over carefully and settled my back against the warm bulk of the dog. We were safe. Someone would come to find us. Had they seen me running behind? Had Eddie told them I'd gone looking for Boomer after all?

I suddenly wondered if there was anyone left to come looking. Had Mom, Henry, and the girls made it to higher ground? Had Eddie? I hadn't seen Dad. What if he'd been swept away by the wave too? What if he was out here floating somewhere? I sat up, sending the raft bobbing unnervingly. Boomer nudged me with his nose.

"Right," I said, scratching his ears. "Move carefully." I peered out across the water but couldn't make out details of anything.

"They better be coming," I said in a small, faint voice. "Somebody's still there, right Boomer?"

He leaned against me, offering some amount of comfort. I turned carefully and wrapped my arms around his broad chest. My teeth began to chatter. Then I lay back down, curling close to Boomer's warm bulk, and I tried not to think about anything. Surely, in a while, I'd have the energy to paddle.

Chapter 3
AFLOAT

Monday, 9:00 p.m.

I lay shivering next to Boomer, staring up at the stars overhead. I knew the constellations—Dad made sure we all did. There was the Big Dipper, faint but clear. And over there, the tail of the Dragon. Where did that put me? My fuddled brain couldn't think it through. I closed my eyes instead. It was easier than thinking.

Boomer's fur was cool and damp against my face. I was so cold, despite his body heat, that I didn't think I would ever feel warm again. We drifted aimlessly amid the floating wreckage—I had no energy to paddle. My head felt too heavy to lift, and my arms and legs were stiff, cramped from staying curled up between Boomer's paws for warmth. With clumsy fingers, I reached out to stroke his thick fur. He nuzzled my hand and licked me as if to remind me he was still there.

The ocean lay strangely calm, like whatever monster had caused the upheaval was sleeping once again. I wondered if the tidal wave would return. I doubted I would survive if it did and wasn't sure I cared. As we dipped and rocked on the gentle waves, droplets of seawater sprayed us both. The ice that formed cracked and splintered whenever either of us shifted.

Our rough raft bumped against something as it bobbed along. I turned my head to look. A scream caught in my throat, then trailed off into a whimper. A person! Face down, dark hair trailing in the water. Part of my mind wondered who it was. I couldn't tell in the dark. It seemed to be a woman, but that was all my befuddled mind could make out.

The next slow wave pushed us away from the body, and I felt a small swell of relief. I looked back up at the sky. The moon still shone, casting a ghostly light over the dark water around me. How long until moonset? How long until dawn? My mind drifted, drowsily. Visions of Winnie, Henry, and Mom played lazily in front of my eyes. I could see them sitting warm around a fire and smiled. Then the happy scene was wiped away by a surge of darkness, and I shifted restlessly.

Sometime later, I noticed that the moon was lower in the sky. Had I slept? Boomer had laid his head on my stomach. The warm imprint of his muzzle remained, but now he was sitting up, alert. Something had caught his attention. I stretched my stiff fingers and tried to move. The dog gave a soft growl and then a chuff. I heard quiet splashing as if someone was paddling in the distance. Slowly, I twisted my neck and peered into the darkness. It took nearly all my energy. Every part of me felt frozen.

A ways off, a single, small flame bobbed and weaved against the darkness. Light? Where did that come from?

Boomer barked once, loud and clear. The light stopped briefly before moving toward us. I wanted to call out, but my voice wasn't working. My throat was so dry, my lips so chapped, that I couldn't force out any words at all. A wordless moan was all that emerged. I doubted anyone could hear me. Voices drifted across the water in disconnected pieces. I struggled to make sense of them.

"That's the Matthews' dog, isn't it?"

"Yes, b'y, I think you've the right of it. What's that with him?"

"A person, isn't it? A child, by the size."

A TERRIBLE TIDE

"Didn't George say his girl was missing? The middle one?"

George? Dad was all right. The relief felt distant, disconnected from my body. The voices drifted closer. Boomer's wagging tail thumped against me, and he gave another resounding bark.

"I see her—the Matthews girl!"

The light hovered over my head now—a kerosene lamp with a flickering flame, held high by a weather-roughened hand. The oil hissed and popped as it moved. There were three men in the dory. One held the lamp, the others manned the oars. They lifted me carefully aboard and tucked a layer of rough sailcloth around me. I smelled tar and tobacco smoke. Home. I settled on the flat bottom of the boat near the bow. Bits of ice flaked off my coat as I moved, swirling in the light of the lamp. I knew these men—they were my neighbors—but in the dark and confusion of the night, I could not think of their names.

"We've got ye, child. You're safe aboard. Now rest, we'll get ye ashore," said one of the men.

"Your mom and dad will be terrible pleased to see you well," said the second man, settling on the bench and taking up his oar.

"C'mon, dog," said the third man. "You done good. Kept her safe. Now come. We'll bring ye home."

33

The dory swayed and sank lower in the water as Boomer stepped in. He squeezed his massive body down in front of me and slurped my face. The dory began moving smoothly through the water as the men rowed with strong, easy strokes. I continued to shiver even with the layer of sailcloth around me. My teeth chattered so loudly, I was sure the whole world could hear them. The men worked quietly but swiftly, moving the boat closer to shore with every stroke of the oars. Half-formed questions skittered around in my brain.

In a short time, we reached a stretch of beach. One man jumped out and pulled the dory up onto the rocky scrum. Boomer leaped out and paced beside the boat, panting, as the men lifted me and set me on my feet. I could barely feel anything, even though there were rough rocks beneath me. Water sloshed in my boots and up my legs. The rough canvas wrapping trailed on the ground behind me.

"Can you walk, girl?" one of the men asked me.

I nodded unsteadily. *I think so.* Did I say that out loud?

Holding the sailcloth like a cloak, I walked forward. My progress was slow and unsteady. Boomer paced beside me, his large paws finding an easier path. I wasn't sure where we were going. We followed the bobbing light of the lamp ahead. The debris I had noticed in the bay was strewn all about onshore as well. I stumbled over broken boards and displaced rocks. At every step, Boomer was there to offer his sturdy back for support. Together, we made our slow way up the path and past the pond. Nothing looked familiar. Was it the darkness or my exhaustion?

Finally, the lamp stopped, swaying slightly as it dangled from my neighbor's hand. I looked up. We were at the steps to the schoolhouse. That, at least, looked much as it always had.

"Come inside, child. You mother's here, and she'll be right pleased to see you."

I went up the stairs and pushed open the door. Inside was very dark, but it was warm and cozy. Someone had a good fire going in the small potbelly stove. My rescuers stepped in behind me, and then Boomer pushed past. He let out an excited whine. His tail began to thump against the wooden benches of the schoolroom. There were people around, but I barely noticed them. A dim figure on the far side of the room turned toward us. The lamp lit only a small circle near the door, but even in the faint light I knew immediately who it was. Mom. Real relief surged through me. I stumbled forward, dropping my sailcloth cloak.

In seconds, I was wrapped tightly in her arms. Tears spilled down my cheeks as she held me close. She's going to be soaked through. Part of me knew the thought was absurd.

"I'm all wet," I said faintly, pushing at her. She didn't need to be wet too.

"Celia, Celia," she murmured against my hair, hugging me tighter. Her voice was half-choked, as if she wasn't sure if she was going to laugh or cry. "Celia, my girl, what happened?"

"I went looking for Boomer," I said in a small, hoarse voice. It was hard to remember everything since I'd seen her last. How long ago was that?

"Yes, girl. Eddie said as much."

"And so I was down by the flakes when the wave came. I saw you on the path up ahead. I couldn't run fast enough, Mom. I tried, I really did…."

"Shh, it's all right, my girl," Mom said, stroking my back as a faint shudder rippled through me. "You're safe now. That's all that matters. Come, we'll get you warm again."

I followed her closer to the stove without resisting. I had a lot of questions, but none of them seemed important enough to ask. Images swirled too, but nothing I could make sense of. When Mom started to strip my wet clothing off, it took me a moment to understand what she was doing and be able to help. From somewhere, she produced a dry nightgown. I pulled it clumsily over my head. It was so nice to feel dry cloth against my skin. I sat down on a soft blanket. As I lay back, my mother covered me with more cloth. I lay cocooned for a long while, still shaking, before I was capable of any more coherent thoughts.

"Winnie?" I asked, sitting up halfway. The sight of her on the path flashed before me, and a shiver ran down my spine.

Mom pushed the still-damp hair out of my face. I couldn't see her as any more than a dark figure against a darker background, but I thought maybe she smiled. "She's fine. We'll talk more in the morning."

I struggled to speak again, to ask about the others. Mom seemed to understand what I wanted to know. "Our family's all right, my girl," she said in a soft, soothing voice. "Don't you worry."

Comforted and warm at last, I drifted off to sleep.

Despite how tired I was, my rest was fitful and broken. There were quiet conversations, the door opening and closing, and people coming and going. Tucked into my blankets, I was warm and cozy, but even so, the cold air from outside was enough to rouse me each time the door opened. Once I woke to my mother snoring softly beside me; the next time she was gone, but Boomer's solid bulk lay along my side. He smelled strongly of fish and seaweed. I patted him gently, rolled over, and fell back asleep.

At some point in the dark of night, a commotion brought me wide awake. There were gruff male voices arguing and much thumping at the door. Dad came in carrying a slight figure, well wrapped in canvas. He set his burden carefully on one of the desks and began to unwind the cloth. By the light of the lamp they'd brought in, I made out a familiar face, topped with a tangle of silvered hair. "Nan?" I gasped, sitting up.

There was a babble of voices talking over one another. No one was paying any attention to me. Mom bustled over to shush them. "It's the middle of the night, George. Can you keep it quiet?" She stopped short when she got there, staring at Nan. Everything about her softened suddenly, and she reached out a tentative hand. "Bea?"

I watched quietly from my corner. What had happened to Nan? I hadn't seen her on the path. Did no one go to help her?

"We found her clinging to the post of the wharf," Dad said, lowering his voice in response to Mom's nagging. "Held on tight to that post and some rope somehow."

Mom pulled the sailcloth away from Nan's slender frame. In the flickering light, I thought I saw her frown. I strained to see what she was looking at. Was Nan hurt? Was that blood on her face?

Nan took a deep breath in and out. "I keep telling these goms, Addie, I'm fine." Her voice was rough as if she, like me, had swallowed mouthfuls of seawater. She was shivering in her thin dress. Was that all she'd been wearing when the wave caught her? Perhaps she'd had a shawl. In normal days she would have.

"You've had quite the shock, though." Mom took a cloth and gently wiped Nan's face. It definitely looked like blood she was cleaning up. I sat up straighter.

"Nothing more than I've been through before. Honestly, they're a bunch of glabauns with all this fussing and worrying. I'll be right as rain in no time." Nan twisted her head away from Mom's attentions. Just like her not to want to be fussed over.

"Maybe so, Bea. But come, let's get you out of that wet dress and warmed up."

Mom had Nan on her feet and was leading her down the narrow aisle toward the stove. I watched in silence as Dad shooed the men back out the door. "My mother's tough as salt cod," he said as the door swung shut behind him. I could imagine the end of the comment even though I couldn't hear him. She'll be all right. I hoped with all my heart that he was right.

I lay awake a bit longer, watching as Mom got Nan settled onto some blankets nearby. She did seem fine, despite her ordeal. I knew how tired I was. However had she managed? She'd been out in the cold far longer than me.

My eyes flickered shut. I fought it, trying to stay awake. Questions whirled in my mind as my exhaustion overtook everything and I fell back asleep.

Chapter 4

DEVASTATION

Tuesday, November 19, 7:30 a.m.

I woke to the light of dawn. The east-facing windows glowed softly, lit by the rising sun. The room was still shadowed, but the light was strong enough for me to see most of it. I sat up, rubbed my eyes, and took stock of the situation around me. It barely looked like the school I knew.

The room was packed—some twenty or thirty of my neighbors crammed into every nook and cranny. A few slept, tucked carefully in blankets, much as I had been. Others lay sprawled in sleepy disarray with no covers to speak of.

Next to me, Nan lay curled on her side, silver hair spread around her like a halo. To my other side, two small children stared wide-eyed from under a desk. Little Mae and Wilfred Rose, the Irvines' grandchildren. The children's mother, Annie, sat huddled on a bench nearby, clutching a shawl around her shaking shoulders. I couldn't help but wonder what had happened. Had the elder Irvines been swept away as I had? Were they still lost? Annie looked a sight, like she hadn't slept a wink while worrying about her parents.

Smoke from the stove hung in the air and made my eyes burn. The small tin bucket, half-full of coal, sat beside the poker. I wondered how much fuel was left.

Looking toward the front of the room, I saw my mother slumped against a desk. Her hair was pulled back from her face into a haphazard knot, nothing like her usual neat bun. There were dark circles under her eyes and smudges on her cheek. Did I look as tired and worn as she did?

I stood and threaded my way through the room until I reached her side. She looked up and smiled.

"Well, here's my girl," she said, reaching out to ruffle my hair. It crackled slightly, flakes of silt floating free. "How are you feeling this morning?"

"Much better," I said. "I felt like I'd never be warm again." At the moment, I was still glad to be warm, but some water to wash with would be very welcome. My entire body felt crusted in brine. Bits of grit and salt and the smell of fish and seaweed clung to my hair and my skin.

She nodded. "Yes, so I can imagine. I've never been stranded a-sea myself, but I've heard enough stories in my life."

"How's Nan?"

Mom looked over at my grandmother's sleeping form. "Fine, so far as I can tell, child. Recovering, much like yourself."

"Where's the others?" I asked. "Where's Boomer?" Part of me didn't want to hear the answers, but I had to ask.

"Your father and the boys are out," she replied. "Looking for people, looking for things. Boomer went with them. I'm sure they've put him to work."

My stomach twisted as I thought of the woman I'd seen floating in the bay. I didn't want to remember anyone like that.

"Are there many people missing still?" I hadn't seen my sisters yet, and I was worried about our neighbors too. Last night Mom had told me our family was fine, but that was before they found Nan. Was she telling me the truth about the others?

"A few. There's full houses floating about, though, and they're still working on searching everywhere."

She looked down at her hands and took a deep breath. Was she hiding something? Worries bubbled in my stomach. I hadn't actually seen Henry or Eddie. Where was Uncle Bert? Viola and Winnie? I was sure I'd seen my sisters on the path last night, just before the wave hit. Were they missing? Hurt? Why wouldn't Mom tell me? My heart began to thump heavily in my chest.

"Mom...," I said, my voice scraping out of my throat. "What's happened?"

She looked up at me, a crease between her brows. Clearly, she was terribly worried about something. Panic rose up in my chest and threatened to choke me.

"It's Winnie," she said at last, in a very quiet, strained voice.

"Oh...," I said faintly, fumbling for a bench to sit on before my knees collapsed.

"Viola's with her, child. She has some experience with nursing, as you should well know. We think Winnie will be fine with some more rest."

"But you don't *know*, do you? What happened?"

My mother scrunched her skirt with her hands. Her eyes darted this way and that. It was obvious that she didn't want to say the next part. "She bumped her head when the wave came in. We were running from the water, out here near the school. Some flying bit of wood clipped her hard on the back of the head, and down she went."

"And then?"

"She hadn't woken yet, last I went to check."

It felt like my spine had collapsed. I tried to breathe. Dark spots swam in front of my eyes, and I lowered my head. "Where is she?" I wheezed.

"Over at the Taylor place, where there's more room." She paused as if weighing what to say next. When she spoke again, it was very hesitantly. "It's one of the few buildings still standing."

My head jerked up and I stared at her, dumb-founded. Whatever did she mean? How many buildings was a few?

"You won't have seen much in the dark last night...." Mom's voice trailed off.

"Enough, I thought."

She shook her head sadly. Then she looked down again as if to gather her thoughts. "Now, my girl, get yourself dressed. There's work to be done for idle hands."

I sat stone-still save for the rapid thumping of my heart. If we were at the school and Winnie was at the Taylors', what did that mean?

"What about our house?" I whispered, nearly choking on the words.

Mom reached out and squeezed my hand. "Gone," she said gently. "But I'm sure you'd figured that already."

I hadn't really thought about it. I searched Mom's face. What were we going to do now? Her eyes were tired, full of worry but not despair. That made me feel a bit stronger. I squeezed her hand back and closed my eyes. Breathing in and out helped me focus.

"Can't I go and see Winnie?" I asked hesitantly.

Mom shook her head again. "Maybe in a bit, my girl. For now, please dress warm and go find your father. He should be down by the beach with the boys. Tell him I need to talk to him."

"All right," I said with a hint of sullenness.

"Celia Rose," said Mom, her voice a warning.

I knew I was being childish. Considering the circumstances, that really wouldn't do. Wasn't I near grown? A girl of thirteen would be a help. I needed to act my age. Even a wash could wait, given everything.

"Yes, Mom," I said, resigned.

A short time later I was ready to go on my errand. My dress had dried overnight. It was dirty but wearable, making me wrinkle my nose as I pulled it on. My stockings, however, were ruined beyond repair. I'd have to go bare-legged. I borrowed a coat and boots. Mine were still damp from my ordeal the night before and hung in the cloakroom, drying.

Outside, the sun shone clear but weak in a pale-blue sky. The air was very cold, snaking around my bare legs as soon as I was out the door. I shaded my eyes and looked out past the pond, down toward the bay. My stomach dropped at the sight, and I felt like I might be sick.

The town lay in ruins, scattered boards and broken pieces of our lives strewn all across the strip of land between the pond and the ocean. Old Mr. Irvine's house stood whole and erect, but across the street from its foundation. It was like some giant's hand had lifted it from its spot and placed it gently down in a new location. I was reminded of my thoughts about monsters.

Closer to the bay, I found half of the sign for Taylor's General Store. The building was gone, and the contents lay scattered all around. Barrels and crates were dumped this way and that, a bolt of cloth half unrolled, and bits of broken glass glinting in the sunlight. Standing upright between two crates was the telephone. One of our links to the rest of the world, broken.

Nearby, a few houses lay on their sides. Everything along the shore was gone—docks, storage sheds, fish rooms, flakes. Two small skiffs sat upright, far from their berths in the bay. One had a broken mast and a trailing sail; the other looked whole, just out of place.

Out in the middle of the bay, a house floated along as if the water were solid ground. I squinted at it. Was that the Hollett place? I couldn't be sure from this distance. A small boat was out near the house with men rowing furiously toward land. What had happened? Curiosity got the better of me, and I picked my way down toward the shore. Broken bits and displaced rocks shifted under my boots. It was hard going, and I had to watch where I placed my feet at every step.

Down on the beach I found my father, Eddie, and some of the other men sorting through damaged crates and barrels. A large piece of sailcloth lay spread out on the rocks, and they were piling useful things on it. Pots and pans, a few dishes, and a crate that was marked as "Medicine." I wondered if any of it was truly useful. Eddie looked up and saw me standing there.

"Ho, CeeCee!" he called. "Feeling warmer this morning, are ye?"

"Good as new," I replied. "Dad, I was sent to tell you that Mom needs to see you."

My father glanced at me. "All right then, my girl. I'll go have a listen." He set down the soggy cotton sack he'd been looking at and headed toward the schoolhouse.

I settled on a large rock outcropping and peered out at the dory on the bay. "Looks like they've found something," I said to my brother.

Eddie looked out toward the boat and grunted. "Likely it's nothing," he said sourly. "Last time it was a crate of ruined tea."

Boomer trotted over just then, followed closely by Henry. Both looked right pleased with themselves.

"Hey! You're up," Henry said, skidding to a stop beside me.

I nodded, reaching out to scratch the dog's soft ears. "What's that you've found?"

"Jar of molasses," he said with a sly smile. "Want some?"

My stomach grumbled in response, but I simply shrugged. "Not without something to spread it on." Boomer nudged my hand, demanding more attention. "He's been fine?"

Henry looked from me to the dog and back before lifting his shoulders. "Seems none the worse for wear. Mom said they found you two together?"

I didn't feel like getting into details. I grunted and continued stroking Boomer's head.

"Well, all right then." Henry sounded huffy, like he'd expected some exciting tale from me. He didn't know, though. He couldn't.

We both fell silent and looked out to sea. The dory pulled closer. The men were rowing as quick as they could. I leaned forward, trying to get a better look.

Maybe they'd found someone hurt. Maybe something exciting. A whole lot of food? Or evidence of the monster I kept thinking about?

Soon they arrived at the beach and pulled the boat ashore. A blanket-wrapped figure lay flat on the bottom between the benches. At first I feared it was someone dead, but the person began to move. She sat up and pushed the wrappings aside. "I said I'm fine, ye great oafs!"

"Now, Maggie, I'm sure you've had quite the night," said Uncle Bert, who was helping her up.

"I slept a good bit of it, Albert Matthews," she replied tartly. "Now let me up!"

"Not tea, hey Ed?" said one of the other men softly. They smirked at each other and continued sorting through the bits and pieces.

Maggie Hollett stepped out of the boat, barefoot and dressed in her nightgown, dark hair uncombed. Had she been abed already when the water rose? That was early for a girl Viola's age. Maybe she'd been sick. Her face was pinched, mouth turned down. I wasn't sure if it was because of the cold or if something else had happened. It surely wasn't her usual expression. She shifted from one foot to the other, curling her toes against the cold. Hadn't she any shoes to put on? I glanced out at her house, then back at her. Maybe not.

"Can you take her up to the school, Celia?" Uncle Bert asked.

I pouted at him for a moment, then remembered that I was not a child and I needed to act like it. "Yeah, sure," I muttered. Going back to the schoolhouse, back inside the warm, close air, was not what I wanted to do. Maybe Winnie was awake, though. I could go up to the Taylors' and check on her.

"Hey, Maggie, come on up to the school. People are there, gathering what they can."

She continued dancing back and forth, lifting her pale bare feet one after the other. She was shivering too. "Yes, let's," she said, stepping quickly as she picked her way up the beach. I trailed after her, looking back over my shoulder. The men were at the dory, pushing it back out into the bay to make another trip. Were there more survivors out there? Bodies of the dead? Or would they come back with just supplies next time?

Chapter 5
NOT A BOAT TO BE FOUND

Tuesday, 12:30 p.m.

Time passed in fits and spurts, long stretches of nothing punctuated by bursts of activity. The men popped in and out, warming themselves in the smoky comfort of the schoolroom. They were taking turns rowing the single usable dory out on the bay, up and down the shore, scavenging whatever supplies they could find. We had some fuel and a bit of food stored in the sheds and kitchens of the houses beyond reach of the flooding. It wasn't much for the entire population of the town.

Most everyone was spending some time at the

school. There weren't many other places to be. Only five houses were still standing, and even they showed the effects of the wave—broken boards and windows, damaged furniture, and lives turned topsy-turvy. Both Maggie and Annie sat staring off into space, leaving the rest of us to watch over the children.

Viola spent nearly all her time at the Taylor place keeping an eye on Winnie, who had still not woken. My heart seemed to be lodged in my throat whenever I thought of her. I struggled to stay busy and keep my mind off my worries. It seemed like there should be a lot to do, and at the same time, there wasn't. I tried, on and off, to amuse the little ones. Nothing seemed to pull them out of their haze. I couldn't blame them for jumping at everything. The fear of more shaking or, worse, another wave was never far from anyone's mind.

Mom and several of the women were taking stock of what resources we had. Several of the young boys, including Henry, were kept busy hauling wood and water. The pond, our usual source of drinking water, was fouled by ocean salt. How far out did they have to go to find a fresh spring? I didn't relish the thought of having to carry water any distance in buckets. If they had a usable sled, it would be easier. Boomer was used to being harnessed up to haul things.

Tired of the smoky closeness of the air inside, I

pulled on my now-dry coat and the borrowed boots and stepped outside. The air had grown colder, and the sky was dark gray with the heavy clouds that preceded snow. There was going to be a storm soon. I wasn't sure who was still missing, but I hoped there wasn't anyone else. Once the snow started, no one would likely be able to keep searching. Fresh snow would help solve the problem of water, though. Melt it in a pot and all's dandy.

I walked carefully along the track from the school toward the bay. Laid out near the foundation of one destroyed house was a row of cloth-wrapped figures. Two tiny ones and six larger. Maggie's mother and two youngest siblings were among them. I shivered. How close had I come to being one of those bodies? How close was Winnie to joining them?

Over at the Taylors', a small group of men gathered beside the house. Someone had found a pack of smokes, and the men were passing one around. The pungent scent of tobacco drifted toward me. I wandered closer.

"Weather's turning," one man said, looking toward the sky. "Won't have a chance to send to Lamaline or Burin once the snow comes. I expect we're too late."

"Maybe if one of the skiffs is usable," said my father, hesitantly. "Be faster than rowing a dory."

"Dangerous though. Like to be a hell of a wind when the storm starts."

"And no one's seen the coastal boat?"

"Not a sight or sound of 'er. She's not due just now, though, is she?"

"No, not till Friday." Dad sighed and took a drag on the twister, then blew a series of smoke rings. "We're on our own, boys. Let's get back to work keeping ourselves alive."

On our own till Friday? That didn't sound good. From what I'd seen, there wasn't enough food for all of us. And what of Winnie and the others who'd been hurt? We needed a doctor. Medicine. We needed them soon.

My father crushed the cigarette under his heel and looked up at me. He smiled, but it didn't reach his eyes. He looked tired.

"Celia," he said, and I walked closer. "How are you, my girl? No ill effects? All's shipshape?"

I nodded, scuffing my toes against the rocks that edged the path. "I'm worrying though. What if Winnie doesn't wake up? What are we going to do to stay warm if the coal runs out? What if there's nothing to eat?" As I spoke, a heavy knot formed in my stomach. So many things could go wrong. The skin of my face was tight. Was it the salt, or some emotion I didn't recognize?

Dad reached out and cupped my chin with his rough hand. He tilted my head up so I had no choice but to look him in the eyes. "We'll manage, girl. Trust that we'll manage."

His expression was earnest. As always, he was a solid presence. His hand was warm against my skin, even in the cold. It helped loosen the tension I'd been holding on to. He pulled me into a tight hug, the wool of his jacket scratching against my face.

"I will, Dad. I will." I leaned into him for a moment, enjoying his solid warmth.

Sounds of movement around me said that the men were moving away. "Coming, George?" one voice called.

Dad stepped back and stroked my cheek with one weathered finger. "You're a strong girl. You've got naught to worry over." He glanced at the other men, who were beginning to move toward the shoreline. "I'll be checking on the skiffs there. Tell your mother I might be headed to Lamaline."

"All right," I said, feeling the knot of worry sitting heavy in my belly. "Be careful."

My father looked me over, head to toe, and gave a final nod before turning away. I stood and watched him go, wondering if he would actually go out on the ocean with the heavy weather coming. We needed help, but at what cost? Would he really risk his life, or the lives of others, to try to save all of us?

The men had gathered around the grounded skiffs

halfway to the beach. They seemed to be checking them over. Looking for holes and leaks, I supposed. They'd need to be sure of the boats before even trying the trip.

I felt a bit better for talking to Dad, but I was still worried about Winnie. Standing back, I looked up at the house. Somewhere inside, my little sister slept. Surely it wouldn't hurt to check on her now.

Moments passed as I worked up the courage to go inside. It wasn't like Nan's house. I wasn't as close to the Taylors, so I wasn't used to coming and going so freely. Would they take it well if I just showed up? I rocked back and forth. The wind licked at my bare legs and sent a chill right up my skirt. I was just about to turn and go back to the school when Boomer appeared, his fur dark against the gray stones and patches of snow.

"Well hello there, boy," I said as he leaned against me. His head was level with my waist, a nice height for scratching along his furry back. Tongue lolling, tail thumping, he leaned so hard it nearly knocked me down.

"Easy, easy," I said, laughing as I stepped back to regain my footing. "What do you think, old boy? Shall we go on in and visit with Winnie?"

His tail wagged even faster, thumping hard against my legs. Together, we stepped up to the door. I pushed it open. No need to knock when nothing was normal, after all. Boomer shoved past me into the kitchen, tail wagging. He wanted to see Winnie too. A sudden howl pierced my skull and made the dog lay his floppy ears flat against his head.

Bessie Taylor stood on one of the kitchen chairs wielding a broom.

"Get out! OUT!" she shrieked. "Get that great dirty lump of fur out of my house!" She was barely taller than me even with the height of the chair beneath her.

I stared at her, wordless. Dirty lump of fur? How dare she call my dog such names. She stared right back, cheeks flushed, and did not let go of the broom. When neither I nor the dog moved, she poked the bristles at Boomer.

"Go on, you. Take your fleas and your smell right back outside."

"He hasn't any fleas!" I said, indignant.

"All dogs have fleas," she replied, scowling at me. "Now get that dog out of here before Gran sees him and we all get a hiding, will you?"

Boomer sighed and looked at me with sad eyes. His tail twitched once, then twice, before stopping. "Sorry, old boy," I said, scratching his head. "Guess you'll have to wait to see Winnie."

I pushed open the door, and he squeezed through.

He didn't go far, just sat down in the snow to the side of the path and took up watch over the house.

Bessie was sitting on the chair when I turned around, looking for all the world as if nothing had happened. "Were you really going to take that dirty, smelly dog into a sickroom?" she asked incredulously.

"Might do Winnie some good to see him," I said. "He looks out for her, you know." I wanted to punch her and wipe the snooty look off her face.

She wrinkled her nose. "I'd be terrible worried about the dirt."

I shrugged. He wasn't really so dirty. "Everyone upstairs?"

"Winnie's in the last room, end of the hall," she said, picking up her embroidery hoop from the table and beginning to stitch. Clearly, she was done talking to me. Fine, then. I'd had enough of her too. Snooty, prissy, annoying Bessie. Thought she was better than me and lorded it over me at school. And just because their family ran the store and my father was a fisherman! Dad had his own family schooner, after all. It wasn't like he was some hired man on someone else's boat.

I passed through the sitting room. Dinah sat near the fire, book in hand. She looked up at me and smiled.

"Was that my lovely sister I heard just now?" she asked, marking her place with a finger.

I nodded.

"Don't you worry, Celia. Gran's gone for a lie down and Mom's down at the school. Nobody need know your dog tried to come in."

"Who's with Winnie?"

"Your Nan and sister, far's I know. Did Bessie tell you which room?"

I nodded again. "Yes, thanks."

"At least there's that," Dinah said, her mouth twisting. "You go on up. Last I saw, Winnie was still sleeping."

Climbing the stairs, I found myself thinking of all the times Bessie had looked down her nose at me. Dinah had never been a snob, which gave me one girl in town I could talk to outside my family. And both of them had always been kind to Winnie. I wrinkled my nose. Even that didn't make up for the way Bessie had just treated me and Boomer.

The hallway was very quiet. Soft snores came from the room at the top of the stairs. Gran Taylor, most likely. I crept past on bare feet, the wood smooth and cool beneath me. Three doors and then one that was propped open at the end. That was the room Winnie was in. I paused in the doorway and peered inside.

Winnie lay in a narrow bed, covers pulled up to her chin. She looked very pale. My breath caught in my throat. Had she died in her sleep? No. There. I could see her chest rise and fall, slow but steady. She was still breathing.

Nan sat on a small wooden stool by the window with a skein of undyed yarn and a pair of knitting needles. Her head was still bandaged. I smiled, a fleeting expression that slid off my face as quick as it had come. Just like her, finding something to do with her hands even though her own house was gone, same as ours. My eyes tingled at that thought. I took a ragged breath. It was just loud enough to catch Nan's attention.

"Come in, child," she whispered, gesturing with her needles toward the sleeping form of Viola. I hadn't noticed her curled in the corner.

I settled carefully on the edge of the bed. Winnie lay very still except for the gentle movement of her breath. I reached out to take one of her small hands in mine and squeezed gently. It was strange to not feel any pressure in return.

"How is she, really?" I breathed, not wanting to wake Viola.

Nan continued knitting, the soft clack of the needles a familiar, comforting noise. "As well as we can hope. Viola says she ought to wake on her own soon."

I swallowed hard, but it didn't clear the lump that

had formed in my throat. "What…?" I struggled to force out the words. "What if she doesn't?"

Nan's fingers stopped, the shapeless bit of wool folding into her lap. "Don't be borrowing trouble, girl. We've enough of it without you inventing more."

Of course she was right, but I couldn't help the worries from bouncing around inside my head. I opened my mouth to say so, but Nan's soft voice interrupted me before I could speak.

"Emily Taylor has invited all of you lot to come and stay. So we can stay close to Winnie, see? I need you to go on down to the school and let your mother know. Then I think you ought to make yourself useful."

I squeezed Winnie's hand one more time. "What do you have in mind, Nan?"

"I know we're still needing things. Why don't you find some of the young scallywags—like Henry, say—and get to gathering what bits of wood you can carry. It'll do if we've no coal to use."

It was a good idea, and I was warm enough now to brave the cold outside again. "Yes, Nan," I said.

She picked up her needles and began knitting again. The soft click-clack followed me down the hall.

Chapter 6

SCAVENGING

Tuesday, 2:30 p.m.

Boomer joined me on the path as I headed back toward the school. When we got there, a few of the younger boys were busy throwing snowballs at each other. Henry turned and lobbed one directly at my face.

"Hey," I yelled. "Don't you be a dirty sleveen, Henry Matthews!" I gathered a handful of snow and hurled it in his direction. My hasty snowball fell apart before it hit anything, so I grabbed for more and took a moment to form it into a more solid lump. The boys scampered around, laughing. Another white missile came my way, but I dodged and it hit the wall instead. I danced to one side, avoiding more snow, and took aim at Henry. He was facing away from me, bent down to make a new ball of his own. As he rose and turned back, I threw mine square at his head. It hit home with a satisfying thud. Henry toppled backward, landing in a patch of trampled snow. His friends laughed harder.

"She's got a good arm, Henry!" called one of the boys.

"Yessir, she does," my brother said with a scowl. "She doesn't play fair, though. What's with not giving a guy a chance, eh?"

I stuck my tongue out at him. His scowl deepened. "All right, all right," I said with a laugh. "Now will you scamps help me gather up some wood? We'll be needing scraps and bits for heating till we get more coal."

"Better than staying in with the women," Henry said, standing up and dusting off his pants.

"Come on, boys. Let's see what we can find."

"Little bits, mind," I called. "Stuff we can break and fit in the stove."

"I get the idea, Celia," my brother yelled back. "You coming or not?"

I scurried after them, my boots slipping on the path where feet had worn a track that was growing icy. Boomer ran ahead, tail wagging. We were heading toward our house. Or what was left of it, anyway. It looked like the cresting wave had lifted our home up off its foundation and then smashed it against the shore. All I could see on our little lot was a bunch of broken boards. Amid it all, the outhouse lay tipped on its side but otherwise intact.

I stared at the scene in disbelief. How was it possible that the house was gone? How had the outhouse not been smashed to pieces? My knees wobbled as I gulped in cold, briny air. The boys stood awkwardly beside me in blessed silence.

"Should we save the big pieces?" Clancy Taylor asked after a few moments, pointing at a spray of whole boards.

Henry and I looked at each other. What to do? As the oldest, I made a quick decision. "Yeah, save the big bits. Maybe we can use them to build a new house."

The boys nodded and began piling the boards more neatly. I began pulling smaller, splintered bits into a heap nearby. Under the wood I found some familiar items. Pieces of our home, our life before the wave.

I wandered, firewood forgotten, and pulled odd items out of the wreckage. One of the beautiful fancy plates, gold edge chipped. A handful of cutlery, dirty but undamaged. We could likely use the forks and spoons once they'd had a good wash. My hairbrush. It too was dirty. Would it be possible to clean it and make it usable again?

And there, tucked under a rock, was Winnie's doll. One porcelain hand was broken, but the rest seemed whole. I picked it up and pulled bits of wood and seaweed out of her hair. The doll's clothes were ruined, stained by salt and dirt, but I thought we could wash out the hair and make her beautiful again. Winnie would be pleased. I grabbed a torn length of cloth—the curtains from the kitchen—and began making a small bundle of items to take back with me.

"Ho, CeeCee!" Henry hollered. "I thought we came looking for wood for the fire!"

I stood upright, twisting the cloth to secure my precious bundle. "We did," I said. "I just found a few other things is all."

Nearby were shattered bits of more plates. We'd barely had a chance to use them. They'd cost Dad a good chunk of his earnings from the fishing season last year. And now they were gone. Everything was gone.

My chin began to quiver and my eyes burned. My fist tightened around the twisted cloth. Tears, hot and salty, spilled down my cheeks. Our home was gone. Our town was gone. Our life was gone. I sank back to the ground, reaching out to brace myself against a rock. How were we going to rebuild from this? Dad seemed sure we'd survive, but I wasn't even sure about that. People were hurt and sick and hungry.

A whimper rose up my throat. The tears were warm on my skin in the cold air. Thoughts tumbled through my mind. What use was a doll, with everything else we were facing? Was my hairbrush really important?

I picked up a small, flat rock and threw it down the path. It bounced off a boulder before landing in soft snow with a muffled thump. All my fear and sadness and anger built up in my chest. With a growl that became a roar, I rose to my feet and hollered at the sky. "IT ISN'T FAIR!" If there was a God, surely this wouldn't have happened. Would it? I sobbed out my anger, shoulders and chest heaving. My nose was clogged, so I wiped it aggressively on my sleeve. I had no idea where there was a hanky.

"Celia?" said a quiet voice from behind me.

My brother stood there, looking at his feet. His cheeks were pink—from the cold, or because he'd been crying too?

"I'm okay," I said, wiping my face dry with my woolen mittens. "Just…fine."

Boomer trotted over and licked my face. He always knew how I was feeling.

"We have some wood," Henry said, pointing at the large heap of broken boards.

"Yes," I said. "That looks a good amount for now."

As we stood there, thick white flakes began falling. The wind, which had been still, began to stir the falling snow and whip it into our faces. "Best get back," I continued, peering up at the sky. I couldn't see the clouds anymore.

The boys had found a large broken board and piled the fuelwood onto it. In the thickening snow, it turned into a makeshift sled. It looked heavy and unwieldy. How were we going to get it moving?

"Now we just need enough rope to make a harness," Ollie said. "I've seen the one your dad used for this big brute. Do ye think we can rig something up?"

"What do ye mean *brute*?" I demanded.

"Yeah, I know the one," Henry said at the same time. We locked eyes, and I grimaced before looking away. No point getting into it with another one of the Taylors over the dog.

"How long is that rope you've got?" I asked, moving to the front of the sled. I lifted the coil of braided hemp, checking its length and condition. It should do. "All right, Boomer. C'mere, boy!"

The dog padded over to me, his large paws spreading wide to help him walk on top of the snow. I looped the rope around his chest and front legs and secured it with a bowline. The knot wouldn't come undone, nor would it tighten so much that we couldn't get it off.

"Ready, Boomer?" I asked, rubbing his fuzzy snout. He leaned into me with his eyes closed, enjoying the attention. I glanced over my shoulder. "All right, boys. Give 'er a push. We'll pull from this end."

Boomer strained against the rope. With creaks and groans, the sled began to move. It was awkward, ungainly, but moving. The boys helped keep the sled on the path as we made our way slowly toward the school. It seemed the best location to pile the wood for now.

Mom seemed relieved to be moving out of the school and into the Taylors' house. I wasn't sure I wanted to spend that much time around Bessie, but I'd put up with her to be closer to Winnie. She was in my thoughts near constantly. Was she going to wake up? Would she be okay when she did?

I spent some of my time watching over her in the quiet room upstairs. Muffled voices drifted up to us as the various residents of the house went about their business. All together there were near twenty of us. Even in a house as big as the Taylor place, we were bound to get on each other's nerves eventually.

As the afternoon went on, I grew restless; I needed to move and do something for a while. When we'd come up from the school, I'd shoved the bundle from our house in a corner of Winnie's room. Now seemed like a good time to deal with the contents. I picked it up and headed downstairs.

"What's that?" Viola asked, glancing at the packet of cloth as I came into the kitchen. She was busy chopping turnips at the counter but set her knife aside to chat with me.

The Taylor girls looked over from the table where they were sitting. Dinah was pink-cheeked as if she'd just come in from outside. She smiled cheerfully at me. Bessie, of course, wore a sour frown like she smelled something unpleasant.

"Some things from the house. I thought we might be able to use them." I set the small bundle down on the counter and untwisted the cloth, revealing its contents.

Viola came closer. "Hmm," she murmured, poking through the small pile. "Needs a wash, eh?"

I nodded. "True, but still useful."

Bessie appeared at my side. She picked up Winnie's doll and looked sideways at me. "Useful?" she sneered.

"Maybe it'll help her wake up," I said. "She's barely ten. Maybe it'll be a comfort." I desperately hoped this was true. She needed to wake up. Or rather, I needed her to.

Viola sighed. "Maybe. It's your job to clean it up though, mind." She pulled out the cutlery and set that on the counter nearby. "Could ye clean these while you're at it?"

"Sure," I muttered. That had been my plan, but Viola telling me what to do made me grit my teeth. Did she not trust me to make my own decisions?

"Get yourself some more snow to melt, eh? What's here is for drinking and cooking with."

"Fine," I snapped. I'd been taking care of things and helping Mom just fine with Viola off to Lamaline. Now she was here and treating me like some baby. "Have we a pail or pot for me to use, then?"

"There's a pail there by the door," Dinah said, gesturing vaguely in that direction. "We'll get the wash cauldron going for you."

"Thanks," I said as I thrust my feet into my boots and picked up the wooden bucket.

Outside, everything was covered in a layer of fluffy snow. The thick flakes were falling heavily, obscuring my vision and making it hard to see anything more than a few feet away. I walked to the side of the house and filled up the pail. It was too cold to stay out for long, but I took a few deep breaths of fresh air before I headed back inside.

The large iron wash cauldron was on the stove when I returned. I dumped the snow into it and paused to consider. It wasn't much. I went back for more. After a few trips I decided there was enough for now and pulled off my boots. Bessie had disappeared, but Dinah and Viola were still sitting at the table. A bowl of peeled chunks of turnip sat on the counter behind them.

"Guess it's turnip for supper," I said, not quite able to stop the sour twist to my words.

"Better than nothing," my sister replied sharply.

"No doubt." I leaned against the counter. "There's no fish to go with it? Or salt beef?"

Viola sighed and leaned forward. "Always thinking of your stomach, Celia." I knew that tone. She was getting ready for a lecture.

"I'm only asking," I huffed as I looked over at the big iron pot. "It's not hurting anyone to ask, is it?"

The snow was clearly melted already because the pot was steaming. I hoped the water was hot, although warm would do. I stomped over to the stove and carefully lifted the pot to tip some of the water into the wash basin. Viola hadn't said anything else. I peeked over my shoulder at her, expecting her to be watching me. Instead, she sat slumped back in the chair. I decided not to bother her with any more questions.

I didn't see any dishrags. We'd need clean cloths for bandages in case of more injuries, so I didn't want to touch what we had. My fingers would have to do. I got to scrubbing and scratching at the dirt and salt crusted on the knives and spoons. It wasn't long before the water was full of silt. I'd need more to clean up Winnie's doll. I laid the flatware out to dry on the windowsill and drained out the dirty water. As I was pouring fresh water into the basin, Dad pushed open the door and hurried into the sitting room. He didn't even shed his coat and boots.

Curiosity got the best of me. I followed him into the other room just in time to hear my mother say, "No, George. It's far too dangerous."

Dad stood up tall, feet planted. "Someone ought to go, Addie. We've no way to get hold of folks in Lamaline or Burin, let alone St. John's. Plus, the coastal boat's not due for days, if she even arrives on schedule."

"It hasn't got to be *you*," Mom said emphatically. "Let one of the boys go. Someone who's not got a family to take care of."

"Like Eddie?" Dad said. He didn't move an inch, but I could tell that he was bracing for a storm.

Mom drew up straighter. "No, not like our Eddie. Someone else!" Her cheeks were flushed and her eyes hard. I was sure she was about to blow up, and I didn't want to be around for that. I shrank back. To my great surprise, she didn't yell. Instead, she crumpled inward, her shoulders slumping and her head hanging. Dad stepped forward and embraced her, his strong arms holding her up. From my spot near the door, I could see Mom's whole body shaking. Was she crying?

I couldn't remember ever seeing my mother cry. Not even when baby Ruthie had died in her sleep, back when Henry had been just a babe in arms himself. Mom always seemed so strong.

My father patted her back awkwardly. He looked over her shoulder and caught sight of me watching them. His brow was furrowed and his mouth set in a thin line. I doubted he had any idea what to do. I sure didn't. I shrugged at him, and Dad turned his head back, pulling my mother closer.

The argument had my thoughts swirling like the snow outside. What had happened in the other towns nearby? Was someone coming? A boat from Burin or even from St. John's? How could they know we needed help? The telegraph line was down. Even if the machine had survived the wave, we'd have no way of sending or receiving messages. The telephone lines were down too, washed away. Travel by boat was dangerous so long as the wind and snow were blowing, and trying to walk to Lamaline along the coast would take hours.

The worries settled in my stomach, weighing me down. I watched my parents as Mom cried and Dad patted her back. It made me feel worse to see that they didn't know what to do either. What were we going to do now?

Chapter 7

WINNIE WAKES

Tuesday, 6:30 p.m.

That night we ate platefuls of boiled turnip. It was filling, true enough, but bland as anything I'd ever eaten. Lucky for us that we had that much, though. The Taylors had stored a bunch from their garden this fall.

I hadn't seen Mom since she and Dad had talked about someone going for help. Like as not, she'd been at Winnie's bedside the whole time. Viola had appeared briefly to grab food, but she'd gone right back upstairs. Nan was in the kitchen, and the kids were crowded into the sitting room. I got up from my spot near the bench and prowled the room restlessly.

Bessie sneered at me from her perch on a chair by the fire. "I'm sure there's something to do in the kitchen if you've got free hands," she said.

I turned my back and ignored her, moving to stand at the foot of the staircase. A small noise—a gasp, or something like it—caught my attention. I strained my ears to see if I could hear anything more, but the chatter of the boys was too loud. My stomach lurched. Had something happened to Winnie? I started up the stairs.

"Something up?" Eddie said, getting to his feet as well.

"I'm going to check. Thought maybe I heard something."

"Come get me if I'm needed, little sis."

"You know I will."

The upstairs hallway was dim and quiet. Muffled voices drifted up from the sitting room. I crept down the hall. I was afraid to make any noise in case I disturbed Winnie, but I was also desperate to make sure everything was all right.

At Winnie's room I stopped, peeking around the half-open door. Mom and Viola were both beside the bed with their backs toward me. Fear prickled up my spine as I considered the possibilities. My throat tightened. She couldn't have died. No way could I deal with that. I stepped forward and the floorboards creaked under my feet.

Viola turned, creating a gap between herself and Mom. She looked exhausted. I caught sight of Winnie's face—pale, but her eyes were open. My breath whooshed out of me, and I grabbed onto the doorframe. Awake! She was awake. Visions of a small, canvas-wrapped body evaporated from my mind. Winnie was going to be all right. A grin spread across my face. I hurried toward the bed.

"Winnie-bear!" I cried, reaching for her hand.

She looked up at me with a smile and blinked. "CeeCee," she whispered. She sounded so tired still. I squeezed her fingers gently. Winnie's dark hair, normally sleek and shiny, formed a tousled tangle about her head. Her eyes were dark and shadowed.

"She's just awake," Mom said, stepping back to make more room for me.

I glanced up. Mom's face was lined with weariness, but there was a sparkle in her eyes that I hadn't seen for a while. Viola hovered behind me, a smile splitting her face as well.

"I'm hungry," Winnie said in her tired, drawn-out voice.

Mom and Viola exchanged a look I couldn't quite make sense of.

"I think a bit of food would be all right," Viola said finally, chewing on her lip. "Just a bit, mind. Was there anything left of the neeps, CeeCee?"

"Maybe some scraps," I said doubtfully. "That pot was right near empty when I got my plate."

Viola huffed, and I drew back. "I wasn't the last, Vi," I snapped at her. "I can't say for sure that there's none."

"Can you look then, please?" she said. She had balled her hands into fists, and her cheeks were pink. She didn't snap back or yell at me, though. That was good. We didn't need to have an argument beside Winnie just now.

"Can't someone else do it?" I was more anxious to stay with Winnie than I was to fill her belly. Surely someone else could get her a plate.

"Just find some food, will you, Celia? It's not so much I'm asking of you!"

"Right then, I'll try," I replied. If there was anything left and no one had started on the washing up, I could bring her some.

Viola herded me out into the hall before I could protest any more. In the dim light, her expression softened. "I know, it's all a racket in here with some dozen or more of us packed in. Plus we've all been worrying over Winnie…."

"All's fine, Vi," I replied. "Be there the once, with whatever I can find for Winnie to eat."

"Thanks, CeeCee. Mom and I do appreciate your help."

She turned to leave, but I reached out to tap her arm. "Does she know where she is? Does she know why?"

Viola's mouth twisted into a frown as she glanced back at me. "Only a bit. Mom told her she was here because there's more room than at our place." She shifted from one foot to the other. "Look, Mom's needing a break, and we don't want to leave her…."

"Go, then. I'll be back in a moment."

I hurried downstairs and through the sitting room, paying no mind to everyone staring after me. I found a clean plate and spoon near the stove. The pot of mashed turnip was nearly empty, but there was a bit left in the bottom. I scraped it all onto a plate, then grabbed a fork from the washbasin before rushing back through the sitting room. Eddie stood up again as I passed.

"Winnie's awake and hungry," I said, pausing at the bottom of the stairs.

"Real glad to hear it," Eddie said. He looked ready to follow me, then stopped as if he was thinking. "I'll wait and go up after she's eaten. Too many visitors might be a bit much right off."

I nodded, balancing the plate against the banister. "Can you maybe find Dad?"

Eddie nodded. "I sure can." He was moving to grab his coat as I continued on my way.

Continued worries about Winnie flooded through me. It wasn't normal to not wake up for a whole day. Something serious could still be wrong. I forced those thoughts away. No point letting myself stew over it, especially if it meant worrying my little sister. I hurried down the hallway. Mom passed me along the way. She saw the plate in my hand and gave me a tired smile.

Back in the tiny bedroom, I found Viola perched on the end of the bed and Winnie sitting up with pillows behind her. I sat down beside her.

"I've a terrible ache in my gut and a headache to boot," Winnie said. "Is that food?"

I held out the plate. "It's cold, I'm afraid."

She took it in her pale, slender hands. "I don't care," she replied, inhaling as she held the dish close to her face. "It smells divine, good as summer rain."

Viola stood, stretching with a pop and creak of her joints. "Thanks for that, Celia," she said. "One less thing for me to do."

I nodded but kept my focus on Winnie. How was she, really? I had so many questions. Was she going to stay awake now? Would she need my help to eat? Viola moved away, her footsteps echoing loudly in the quiet of the room. Winnie, meanwhile, was taking little bites of the cold mash. Every bite came with a small purr of pleasure.

We sat in silence while she ate. After a while—I couldn't tell how long—Winnie set the plate down beside her on the blanket.

"That was delicious. Thank you, CeeCee. My stomach doesn't feel like it's gnawing through, now." Her color looked better in the lamplight. She didn't look white as the snow outside anymore.

"I'm glad," I replied, patting one of her small hands. "How's your head?"

She grimaced, then rolled her shoulders in a shrug. "Pounding. Not as bad as when I first woke, I'd say." She picked at the covers, fingers moving restlessly. "Where did Mom go? She was here when I woke. And where are Dad and the boys? I haven't seen them."

"Mom's around, downstairs, I think. Eddie was in the sitting room when I came up, and I'm sure Henry's around…." Viola came and sat beside me at the end of the bed. My eyes met hers, and she gave the slightest shake of her head. I nodded. Best not to say too much.

"Oh, is there a party?"

"Just a small gathering," Viola said soothingly. "Too much of a hurly-burly for you just now, though."

Winnie nodded, careful not to move her head too quickly. "Yes, I think that would make my head pound worse." She sighed then, a soft exhalation. "I'm restless," she said. "I want to get up."

I wasn't sure about that, so I glanced at Viola. My older sister's face was hidden by the shadows of the dancing lamplight, but she held herself very still except for the slight tap of one finger on her chin. "All right," she said at last. "Careful, now. And only upstairs. No need to risk the stairs just yet."

We helped Winnie to her feet, pulling the covers clear of her legs. She gripped my hand tightly. "All right?" I asked, squeezing her fingers gently in return.

"Yes," Winnie said. "Just…I can tell I've been abed a while. My head's a bit spinny."

"Do you need to lie down again?" Viola asked, moving closer.

"No, it's all fine. I think I'd like to walk a little."

I stayed close by, ready to steady her if she needed it. Winnie moved slowly, placing her feet carefully so as not to stumble or trip. One hand rested on my arm. Her crippled leg made the process even slower. We made several trips up and down the hall. Finally Winnie stopped, rubbing at her temples and breathing heavily.

"I think I need to lie down again."

I helped her settle back onto the bed. "How's your head?" I asked anxiously.

"Hurts," she replied, eyes closed. She leaned back against the headboard and took several short, shallow breaths. "Hurts a lot, actually."

There were pills for that—Nan took them sometimes when her rheumatism got bad—but I didn't know if the Taylors had any. And even if they did, I wasn't sure how to tell them from any other kinds of medicine. Small white pills were all the same if you didn't know what to look for. I bit my lip. No way I wanted to take a risk and give her something wrong. Maybe Viola would know, but she had disappeared for a moment. It would have to wait.

"Lie back," I said softly. "Let's see if rubbing your head helps any." I shuffled around so that I sat behind her, my back pressed against the wall. She leaned into me with her head nestled in my lap. I stroked her forehead and temples, adding light pressure with my thumbs. I didn't want to press too hard in case that made the pain worse.

"I don't feel well," said Winnie suddenly. She was back to looking pale.

"What's wrong?" I asked in alarm.

"I think I'm going to yuck," she replied weakly, struggling to sit up.

"Is there something...?" I looked around wildly and caught sight of the empty plate, lying abandoned in the corner beside the bed. I scrambled to grab it, hoping that she wouldn't sick up before I could get there. I really wasn't sure I could handle cleaning that up. As I shoved it into Winnie's hands, Mom opened the door and came in. Dad's sturdy frame stood behind her in the shadows of the hallway. I felt a rush of relief just as Winnie began to heave.

Chapter 8

THE COASTAL PATH

Wednesday, November 20, 7:00 a.m.

I slept next to Winnie that night, rousing at every small movement she made. Even though I didn't sleep well, I woke feeling happier than I had in days. She had woken up. She was going to be all right.

The small room felt very crowded with Winnie and me in the bed and Viola curled up in a nest of blankets on the floor. I pushed back the covers and stepped out of bed. My toes curled up from the cold boards. After a moment's hesitation I stood, then tiptoed out of the room. No need to wake either of my sisters.

Out in the hallway, I stopped to listen. A few faint noises came from downstairs—low voices and quiet clinks and bangs. Someone was awake and probably making breakfast. My stomach rumbled. I headed down the stairs to have a look.

Nan and Gran Taylor were both in the kitchen. They sat at the table with a steaming teapot perched between them. Neither woman spared a glance for the other, but Nan looked up at me with a smile when she heard me come in.

"Good morning, Celia," she said, gesturing to the chair next to her. "Come have a sit and a sip of tea."

I joined them at the table. Tension hung heavy between the two old women. It made me wonder what they'd said before I woke. No point in asking, though. Nan would be like to tan my hide if she thought I was speaking out of turn.

Instead, I decided to deal with my grumbling stomach. "Is there something to eat?" I asked. My voice sounded plaintive despite my best efforts not to be a whiny child.

Nan chuckled warmly, but I noticed Gran Taylor glaring at me. "We've still some neeps, child. Nobody's ready for making much more quite yet."

I sighed softly but smiled anyway. "That'll do."

A short time later I went outside to stretch my legs

and check on Boomer. The wind nipped at my nose and cheeks, but the sun shone bright overhead. Toward the bay, a few men clustered around the damaged boats. Broken bits of the village still floated out in the bay, bumping up against chunks of ice that had been dislodged by the force of the wave. No one seemed willing to take a boat and go off to Lamaline, or further. Not even today when the snow had stopped.

I had a thought. I stopped near the pond to consider the plan. Boomer paddled over and climbed out of the water, fur dripping. He shook. Droplets sprayed in every direction, splattering me. I giggled.

"What do you think, boy? Should we go see how it is down Lamaline way? No one else seems willing, and we sure do need some help here."

The dog sat silently in the snow, then snuffled at my hand.

"Of course, you'd come with me," I said, scratching behind his ears.

"Come where?"

I spun, heart hammering. Henry stood there, hands shoved in his pockets, staring at me.

"Oh," I said, "I was thinking."

"Yeah—thinking of going somewhere," he replied. He waited, hazel eyes narrowed.

"Maybe Lamaline," I admitted, after a long pause. "Dad and the other men said someone ought to go, but they haven't."

Henry kicked at a pile of snow, sending a spray of white into the air. It made me think of the spray of water when waves crashed against the rocks in the bay.

"Could be dangerous," he said.

I nodded and continued scratching Boomer's ears.

"You shouldn't go alone," Henry said, removing his hat and shaking off the layer of snow that had gathered there.

"You offering to come?" I asked.

He grinned at me. "Could be fun."

"Should we let someone know where we're going?"

Henry shook his head. "I think no, CeeCee. Who're you going to tell who won't just say don't do it?"

"Right," I said, tugging my scarf tighter around my neck. "Need anything else?"

"I'm shipshape," he replied, eyes alight with excitement.

We followed the tracks away from the house. Just beyond the pond the path forked. West led to Lamaline 'round the point at Point au Gaul. Eastward was Lord's Cove. I looked at Henry.

"If the wave hit all along the coast, I can't see as how we'll get any help at Point au Gaul or Lord's Cove."

"True," he said, facing westwards. "Best bet's to go as far as Lamaline."

The path along the coast was rough at the best of times. In the snow, it was even harder going. We slogged through the drifts, stopping now and then to breathe in the cold, salty air and take a rest. Boomer walked along beside us, his large paws helping him stay on top of the snow in places where we broke through.

"Should've brought a sledge," Henry muttered as he pushed through one particularly large pile of snow.

"Don't think there is one," I replied, panting as I stopped behind him.

He made a noncommittal noise and, pointing further along the path, he said, "Think the bridge is out up there?"

I peered ahead. It was hard to tell for sure. The path had many small bridges that crossed the marshy areas and some of the narrower gaps. I knew of one near the berry patch we came to most summers. Was that where we were now? Yes, I recognized that stand of trees to our right and the shape of the boulders there along the shore.

"Let's go see," I said, taking the lead and pushing through the snow.

Henry followed, and Boomer paced along beside him. As we drew close to the tiny stream with its plank bridge, it became clear that the bridge had, indeed, been washed away.

My brother came to stand beside me and examined the slope. "Not going to be an easy crossing," he said, shoulders slumping.

The wind came up just then and dusted us with icy pellets. I wiped my face, clearing my eyes.

"I'm not sure we should keep going," I said, doubt creeping into my heart.

"I'm no quitter," he replied stoutly. "See there, a branch is down just along the edge of the rise. We can use that to make a new bridge."

"Henry," I said, my doubts growing. "That's not safe. It's already getting late. We're never going to make it all the way to Lamaline like this."

He looked over his shoulder as he trudged toward the fallen branch. "We never will if you keep on like that, Celia. Now come and help me, will you?"

I took two steps toward Henry before he slid out of sight down the slope. When I got to the top of the rise, I could see him lying in a tumbled heap at the bottom. My heart nearly stopped. "Henry?" I called hesitantly.

My brother moved slowly, untangling his arms and legs and getting to his feet. "I'm all right," he called back. "Bumped around something fierce, but not hurt badly."

I wasn't sure of that. He seemed to be limping as he clambered carefully up the slope. When he got to the top, I made him stand still for a look over.

"Did you bump your head?" I asked, gnawing on my lip and thinking of Winnie.

"Nah," he said, raising his arms over his head to check how well he could move them.

His clothes were covered in snow, even matted down in places. When I got to his legs, I realized that he'd torn his pants in the fall.

"How's the leg?"

Henry flexed into a half-seated position, then straightened again. "It's fine. Just a scratch, I'm sure."

"We ought to go home," I said firmly. I'd make him listen to me if I had to. Time to be the big sister, like Viola always was to me. "You're in no shape to keep along. Let's get you home and have Mom take a look, just to be safe."

He didn't argue, which told me that he was hurt worse than he wanted to let on. We trudged back along our tracks toward home. I kept the lead, letting Henry follow in the packed-down snow and lean on Boomer as we went. It seemed to be taking forever. Maybe it was the worry, or maybe Henry was just moving that much slower. Thankfully, the weather stayed clear. I couldn't imagine walking back through even more snow.

As we walked, the sound of hoofbeats rang through the air. Boomer barked once in warning. I glanced behind us, past Henry's slouched shoulders, to see a well-wrapped figure on horseback leap over the stream. The horse neighed as his rider pulled up beside us.

"What're you lot doing out here?" The voice was rough but female. I stared at the woman on the horse. Surprise had stolen my voice.

"We're from Taylor's Bay," Henry mumbled, leaning against Boomer's solid black bulk. "Went walking along the coast to see if we could get to Lamaline. Things at home…well, it's not so good."

The woman reached up to pull her scarf down. Her eyes were bright and kind, in a round face pink with cold.

"Well you'd best be heading back," she said quietly. "It's no better from here." She paused. "I'm Dorothy Cherry. Lamaline's where I started this trip. It's bad all along the way, and I'm looking to see how I can help."

"Help?"

Dorothy Cherry looked down at me and smiled. "I'm a nurse, see. And I know there's people been hurt."

My heart thumped in my chest. Maybe she could take a look at Winnie, then. Maybe she'd know if we had something to really worry about. I opened my mouth to mention it, but before I got a word out, Henry let out a low moan and slumped to the ground.

"Are you all right, b'y?" Nurse Cherry asked, sliding down from the horse's back.

"He had a fall, just back there," I replied, hurrying to kneel beside my brother. "He said it was nothing!"

"It is nothing," he said, panting slightly.

"Looks like it might be something," the nurse said, pursing her lips. "Can you get up on the horse, lad? Might be easier going than trying to slog through all of this."

She helped Henry to his feet, then boosted him up on the horse's broad back. He stared at me, wide-eyed, and clung to the saddle. I didn't think he'd ever been on horseback before. No one nearby had ever had one for us to ride.

The nurse glanced at Henry's leg, frowning slightly. She ran her fingers along the slit he'd made in the fall and tutted quietly to herself.

"We'll take it slow and steady," Nurse Cherry said after a moment, turning to me. "Lead the way, if you will."

I headed off toward home with Boomer trotting beside me. Nurse Cherry led the horse, which picked its way carefully through the snow. High up on the horse's back, Henry kept up a stream of mutters. Was he praying or cursing? I couldn't hear him clear enough to tell. Finally, we rounded the path beside the pond and headed to the big house. No one seemed to be around, and I felt bubbles of panic rise. What if Mom wasn't in when we got there?

We banged our way into the kitchen, leaving Boomer outside. Mom and Viola sat by the window, talking in low voices. They looked up when we came in. Henry limped over to them with me trailing behind. Nurse Cherry stopped to tie the horse to the railing but followed us inside after a moment.

"What's happened, child?" Mom said to Henry, taking in his rumpled, torn, and snowy appearance. She spared a look for the nurse but her focus quickly returned to Henry.

"Took a tumble," he replied. "Scratched my leg pretty good."

"Let's have a look then," she said briskly. "Up you get."

Henry clambered up onto the table and extended his leg. Mom carefully pushed the pant leg up past his knee, exposing the wound. The sight of it made me squeamish. His "just a scratch" was in fact a long, shallow cut that ended in a deeper slice near his ankle. The skin was ragged all the length of the cut like it had been hacked at, not cut cleanly as if with a knife. I looked up, away from the sight, and met Henry's eyes. They were wide and teary above red cheeks and trembling lips.

I reached out to squeeze his hand. "It's nothing, remember? Just a scratch."

His lips twitched, just the ghost of his usual smile, and he squeezed back. "That's right," he said. "Nothing but a scratch."

Nurse Cherry came to stand nearby. "Ooooh, that's quite the cut you have there. No wonder walking was such a chore!"

Mom looked up from her examination of Henry's leg. "And who's this?" she asked, glancing at me.

"We met her on the path toward Lamaline," I said, feeling a small stab of guilt in admitting where we'd been. Mom didn't comment or ask what we'd been doing, though. I was glad for that.

"Dorothy Cherry. I'm a nurse, come from Lamaline along the coast to see what help I might offer." She paused, looking down at Henry. "Brought the lad back a-horseback when he was having trouble walking in the snow. Might I have a look?"

"Nurse, you say? Perhaps you've an idea what to do here, then." Mom stepped sideways to let Nurse Cherry move closer.

The nurse hummed softly to herself as she worked. I looked down, briefly, to see her poking and prodding at the skin around the cut. Henry gasped and tightened his grip on my hand. It must be hurting more than I'd thought.

"Well," Nurse Cherry said after a while. "We're going to need a few things."

Viola hovered nearby. "Cloths?" she asked, stepping closer.

Mom nodded. "Clean ones. Very clean. And boiling water."

"Yes," the nurse said, stepping back from Henry. "I have a few things in my pack that might help. We'll need to do something to help keep that cut from getting infected."

"We'll also need some way to close it," Mom said, frowning. She tapped her fingers on the hard surface of the table. "Celia, please go and find me a good gob of pine sap and put it in a clean pot. An old one if you can; we won't be able to use it for food after."

"Ah, the sap's good. Helps with infection," Nurse Cherry said. She gave me an encouraging smile. "I ought to have a bit of something to help clean it too."

Henry reluctantly let go of my hand. He took a long, steadying breath and shifted his leg.

"You, my boy, stay where you're at. We'll be needing the light to do what needs doing." Mom's tone was clear—she'd tolerate no argument.

He stopped moving. "How long…?" he said in a very faint voice.

"As long as it takes, child. Now get yourselves to moving please, girls!"

Viola bustled off to find the clean cloths and hot water. I grabbed a small, battered pot from its hook above the stove and headed outside. Nurse Cherry was already out there, untying the pack from her horse. Scrawny pine trees grew on the rocky ridges outside of town. I pulled my slouchy knitted cap down over my ears and hurried in that direction. Partway there, Boomer trotted up and fell in beside me.

"Hey, boy," I said, pulling off one mitten to scratch his ears. "Where did you go?"

Of course there was no answer. His fur was dry, save for a bit of snow damp, so he hadn't been in the water. Had he eaten? He was fully capable of catching a few fish, but not without getting wet. Was he catching birds or mice instead? I'd never thought of him as that good a hunter. The one thing I hoped he wasn't catching was chickens. The Taylors had a few, but I doubted they'd take kindly to sharing them with the dog.

We hurried along together and reached the small stand of trees in a few minutes. I needed a tree with broken branches that had started to heal. The pine sap would collect there and begin to harden. I hoped to find a recent break so the sap hadn't hardened too much, since that would just take a lot longer to melt and soften enough to use.

The trees were small but hardy. They gripped the rocky ground with a web of roots, finding tiny cracks to dig into. The wave had not swept up this far—no debris or wreckage blocked my way. The snow and wind, on the other hand, had broken off a few branches. It took only a short time to find what I was looking for in the cracked *V* of a low-hanging branch. I took off both mittens and stuffed them into my pockets before working the sticky golden glob of sap loose from the bark. As I dropped it into my pot, fresh sap oozed over the exposed inner wood. There would be more there tomorrow if we needed it.

My hands were cold without the mittens but sticky from the sap. I didn't want to put the mitts back on when they'd just get sticky, in turn, and then need washing. I left them in my pockets and gripped the pot's metal handle. If I was quick, it should be all right.

Back at the house, I hurried inside and plunked the pot directly on the stovetop, next to a steaming cauldron. It wasn't boiling yet. Viola bustled over to check on it and started chattering.

"Best get another pot, Celia, and make a warm bath for that sap. If it gets too hot it can burn quick."

That was sound advice. I remembered seeing a pine-sap torch one year at Christmas. Once lit, the flames had taken very quickly. We didn't need that inside the house.

In just a few minutes I had a second pot of snow melting on the stove. Someone—Viola or Mom, I assumed—had moved the pot of sap off the heat for now. The larger cauldron bubbled gently. Mom looked over and saw the steam. "Bring that here, Celia child. And find a cup or ladle, please."

I quickly followed her instructions, catching the worry from her rushed words. Should I have been more worried? Once I'd gathered everything, I sat down on a chair by Henry. He fumbled for my hand, and we looked up at Mom and Nurse Cherry.

Viola appeared beside me with a small cup of pungent-smelling screech. Wherever had that come from? Gran Taylor must have had a stash. I couldn't quite imagine Mrs. Taylor drinking it.

"Here, drink up," Viola said to Henry. "It'll help numb the pain a bit."

He took the cup, held it up to his lips, and wrinkled his nose. "Smells awful," he complained.

"Drink, lad. It does help some," Mom said quietly. "Vi, have you the strap as well?"

My sister nodded and held out a small scrap of

leather. Henry scrunched up his face, then downed the whole cup of liquor in one go. He came up coughing and spluttering. "Tastes worse'n it smells!"

"It'll be well, lad," Mom replied. She eyed the water closely and picked up the battered ladle. "Now put that strap in your mouth, will you, Henry?"

He opened his mouth to protest, and Viola took the chance to slip the narrow band of leather between his teeth. "Bite down if you feel like you need to scream," she advised him. Her eyes glinted with amusement as he glared at her.

I couldn't watch what the women were about to do, but I couldn't leave either. I gripped Henry's hand firmly in mine and watched out the window. Boomer trotted past like he was on a mission. Clancy Taylor, followed by his father and a few other men, headed in the other direction. Small splashes told me that someone was pouring the hot water over Henry's leg. He squeezed my hand hard, jerking and grunting a few times, but he did not scream. When I took a quick glance at his face, his eyes were closed and he was breathing hard—quick puffs of air, not quite soundless. Perhaps it helped him deal with the pain? I didn't want to think about that and jerked my gaze back to the window.

Viola brought over the pot of softened sap. I looked up at her in surprise. Who had set it to melting? My attention had been so focused on Henry that I hadn't noticed.

"All right now, lad," Mom said in her best no-nonsense voice. "We'll seal you up with this and then get it all wrapped tight. Hold on, m'boy."

Viola, Mom, and Nurse Cherry talked quietly to each other as they worked. Henry held himself very stiff and did not let go of my hand. I was torn between wanting to watch what they were doing and not wanting to look at the raw wound on his leg. My curiosity quickly won out over my squeamishness. Viola held the ragged edges of skin tight together while Mom poured the liquid pine sap over the cut. It quickly began to harden again, holding the edges of skin together and protecting the tender insides. A short time later, Nurse Cherry was wrapping Henry's leg in strips of cloth for bandaging. His grip loosened, and he began to sag.

"Henry?" I said softly, standing up.

"I'm some tired," he replied, his voice slurring as he slumped against me.

Chapter 9
DUCK STEW

Thursday, November 21, 10:30 a.m.

Mom and Mrs. Taylor had managed an uneasy truce between them in the house. It was strange to see my mother defer to anyone, but when it came to decisions affecting everyone, she did just that. When it came to our family, though, she was as firm and fiery as ever. And she wasn't shy about barking orders at the Taylor girls when their mother and grandmother weren't around.

We'd been up with the sun again, seeing Nurse Cherry off on the next part of her journey. She was headed down the coast toward St. Lawrence and then Burin. She'd taken a look at Winnie after helping with Henry's leg, frowning and leaving instructions that she only take short trips out of bed for a few days. A small stock of aspirin tablets had been cautiously handed over to Mom, who kept them in a battered tin in her apron pocket. Everyone knew they had to be used only when truly needed. With Nurse Cherry's news of damage all along the coast at least as far as Lamaline, we had no idea when we might be able to get more. She'd not had many details to share about who might be lost, or dead, or missing, and some of our neighbors were worried sick about friends and family in the other towns nearby.

As the sun rose higher in the sky, Dinah and I sat sorting through random bits of clothing at my mother's request. It seemed as if everyone who had anything extra had dropped it off to share with those who had none to speak of. I'd rather be doing something else, but Mom's expression had left no room for questions or arguments. Even Dinah had quickly agreed to the task. I guessed we were looking for fresh outfits for everyone, or as many as we could manage. Definitely a full set of clothes for those like Maggie, who'd come through the disaster with only a nightgown.

We could hear a low rumble of voices from the kitchen as we worked—Nan, Mom, and Gran Taylor were discussing the food situation. We had so many mouths to feed—the seven of us, eight Taylors, plus Maggie Hollett—that it was really becoming an issue. All the dried cod had washed away, and the bay was so torn up, no one had been able to catch anything fresh. The folks crammed into the few other buildings weren't faring any better.

"How's Henry?" Dinah asked. "I haven't seen him today."

"He's got a right dreadful cut on his leg. Mom thinks it must have been a nail in the scrap from the bridge that did it. She had to fix him up once we got him home. Although I'm sure she was glad for the help of a real live nurse."

Dinah shuddered delicately. "It sounds awful. I'm glad there was someone experienced to help too. Did she have much to say about Winnie?"

I nodded, thinking of how queasy I'd felt looking at the cut. "Henry had a good measure of screech to help him through it. As for Winnie? Not a lot."

Dinah chuckled as she held up a child-sized dress and shook it. The creases remained stubbornly in place. "And how long did he sleep for, after?"

I laughed ruefully, smoothing out a worn blue shirt. "Till this morning, I think."

She nodded sagely. "I remember once when our

Ollie got into the screech. Mother was furious. He slept for hours and woke with his head throbbing like the waves against the rocks."

"Oh, poor Henry," I said. "He must feel worse from that, I suppose, than from his leg!"

I hoped it wasn't as bad as all that. As annoying as my brother was, I still didn't have an ill wish against him. I hadn't been around when Mom and Viola checked on the cut this morning. There'd been no talk of it that I'd heard, so it seemed things must be all right there. Viola was upstairs with the kids just to make sure. I wouldn't be surprised to find her grabbing a few extra winks given how much she'd been caring for everyone.

Mom poked her head in from the kitchen just then. "Girls, leave that for now, will you please? We could use some help here in the kitchen."

Dinah and I exchanged a confused look over the basket of clothing. I shrugged and laid the shirt I was holding on top of the pile so it wouldn't wrinkle so badly again. Dinah gave the dress another look over, then sighed and shoved it back into the heap. "I think it's a lost cause without ironing," she said.

I had to agree. An iron or a thorough washing.

In the kitchen, the women were gathered around the table. Eddie lounged by the door with a cheeky grin on his face. Whatever was he looking so pleased about?

I looked from him to the table, where I saw the reason for it. A pair of ducks, whole and feathered. It was near impossible to believe, save for the fact that the birds were right there.

"Late in the season for ducks," Dinah remarked, mirroring my own thoughts.

Eddie's grin widened. He seemed mighty proud of himself.

Mom gave him one of her serious looks, and his grin slipped. "And what shall we do with them, feathers and all?"

He stopped leaning against the doorjamb. "I suppose I can clean and gut them."

"It would make them easier to cook," Mom agreed in a level voice.

"Yes. Well, I'll be outside taking care of the birds then."

My stomach rumbled hungrily, and thoughts of roast duck danced through my mind. The birds would make a nice change from the steady diet of turnip and cabbage we'd been eating. Tender, juicy duck meat, dripping with juices from the roasting pan....

Nan tapped her foot against the table leg. "I think duck stew will be the best," she said. "We'll get more food for all that way."

I sighed aloud. I couldn't help it. Mom gave me a sharp glance.

"Sorry," I mumbled, looking down at my toes, feeling deflated. The shimmering image of steaming roast duck faded from my mind. "What will we need to go with it, Nan?"

"We've still some turnips in the shed. See what potatoes are left too. And onions. Only one, though. The flavor will be nice, but we don't want to use them all up."

Gran Taylor nodded along with Nan's list. "There's some dried herbs too. Dinah knows where, don't you girl?"

"Yes, Gran. Maybe some sage?"

"That should do," her grandmother replied.

We pulled on our coats and headed out into the bright, frigid day. The cold cellar was a small shed just to the left of the house. The Taylors kept a fair-sized garden in the warmer months and so were able to put away vegetables, both fresh and dried, for the winter.

Dinah pushed open the door, and we stepped into the dim interior. Slightly musty, earthy smells flowed into my nose. As my eyes adjusted, I could see a few strings of onions hanging from the rafters. Barrels lined the walls, lumpy shapes only visible when I peered into their depths. Potatoes, like Nan suggested. And turnips—always turnips. A few dusty jars were perched on narrow shelves above them. The shed looked nearly empty.

I gathered a handful of potatoes from the bottom of one of the barrels.

"Grab a basket," Dinah said over her shoulder as she picked through bundles of dried herbs in the corner. "Over there, by the door."

I found a fair-sized basket and dropped the taters into it. Outside the open door, there was some rustling and snuffling. Boomer, I thought to myself. That dog did insist on hanging around the foodstuffs, always in hope of getting some scraps. He'd have to fend for himself more at the moment, though—there wasn't enough to share with the great oaf. I stepped outside to shoo him off. "Get on with you, Boomer," I said, then stopped dead.

The animal before me was indeed large and black, but it was not a dog. It was a fair bit larger than Boomer—a stocky figure with a very thick coat, long tapered muzzle, and rounded ears. Its small eyes peered around in the bright light, and it grunted. I stood frozen, breath caught in my throat. How long had it been since there'd been a bear in town?

My heart pounded in my chest as the bear sniffed the air. It snuffled and snorted, then reared up on its hind legs. It stood nearly as tall as the edge of the roof, towering far above my head. I muffled a scream. It took every bit of control for me not to turn tail and run. Had it noticed me, or was it just looking for food? I tried to gather my scattered thoughts. What had Dad said to do if I ever ran across a bear?

Behind me, Dinah gasped. I glared at her over my shoulder—was she going to attract its attention? Before I could say anything, she began to shriek. I took two quick steps back inside and scrambled to close the door. Dinah's piercing cries made it hard to think. The door stuck on the uneven floor. I pushed with all my strength, but it would not budge. My sweaty hands began to slip on the worn wood. My heart pounded so hard that I could barely hear anything else. The sound muffled even Dinah's panicked screams.

All the noise seemed to be confusing the bear. It swung its heavy head back and forth, huffing loudly. I threw my shoulder against the door and bounced back, but the door scraped a few inches across the floor. The bear lowered itself to all four paws and sniffed toward the half-open door. No way was I letting it into the shed. This was *our* food. We didn't have much, and I sure wasn't going to share it with some bear! I took two steps back and threw my weight against the door again. Finally, it came free of its snag and slammed shut.

Taking a few shaky breaths, I stood tall and straightened my skirt.

Dinah was huddled against the back wall. In the darkness, I could just make out her small form crammed in between some boxes.

"Is it gone?" she asked, her voice quavering.

"Not yet, but it can't get in."

"Are you sure?"

I wasn't sure of anything. My legs felt like jelly, and my heart was ready to burst through my chest. I was aware of the hulking form of the bear outside—it was still huffing and whuffling nearby. Dinah didn't want to hear all that, though. She wanted to hear that everything was fine. I prayed silently that it *would* all be fine and took several steadying breaths. It wasn't a sin to tell a small lie at a time like this, was it?

"It can't get in. And so it will be gone soon enough. I'm sure of it."

"It's some size of a bear." Dinah uncurled herself and hesitantly inched out from between the crates.

"Yes, it sure is. But it would have to be real desperate to keep trying to get in here." I walked a few steps across the shed and sat down next to her.

Outside, the bear grunted. The sound came from right behind us. Dinah squeaked in surprise and scooted closer to me. Her eyes were very wide in her pale face.

"It's circling the shed," she whispered.

"Yes, so it seems. But it can't get in no matter where it is." My voice trembled a bit, and I struggled to control it. "Can you imagine how silly that old bear must look, hunting for vegetables? Imagine his bear-mates saw him."

Dinah gave me an odd look, so I forced a grin. Making someone laugh was a sure way to make them feel better.

"I mean, think about it. A savage animal scrounging 'round people?" She looked more nervous than amused, so I tried again. "Imagine his family, right? Watching him? Instead of hunting like a proper bear."

Just then the bear grunted again and bumped against the wall with a solid thud. Dinah screeched and clutched my arm. Her fingers dug in so hard that my hand started to go numb. I could hear the bear breathing on the other side of the thin wooden wall. I stared at Dinah, my fake certainty trickling away. It was all I could do not to add my shrieks to hers.

A booming voice rang out suddenly. Other voices joined in. They began to hoot and holler and make a terrible racket. The bear let out a series of grunts followed by several heavy thumps. The voices grew louder, wordless shouts designed to frighten the animal away. I heard another loud exhale and one or two more grunts, each further away from us. They'd done it! The bear was leaving.

Both of us jumped, nerves jangling, when the door crashed open. Light spilled in. A dark figure filled the doorway. I couldn't see who it was.

"Celia? Dinah?" Eddie called. "All shipshape in here?"

I felt a rush of relief as I clambered to my feet. Dinah held on to me and pulled herself up to stand beside me. "We're here. We're fine." I stumbled forward, tugging Dinah along with me, and fell into Eddie's arms. He wrapped us both in a fierce hug. Tears stung my eyes, although I didn't know why. I wasn't hurt; everything was fine. There really was no reason to cry.

"Come along inside, girls," Eddie said, his voice a comforting rumble. "Clancy and Ollie will come back and gather what we need."

Chapter 10
MAKING A GOOD TIME

Thursday, 7:30 p.m.

After our dinner of duck stew, everyone settled into small groups around the house. Winnie, Dinah, and I sat on the narrow bed, playing a game of scat. A small stack of cards lay on the quilt between us, and we each peered thoughtfully at the cards in our hands. My own hand held three hearts, but all small ones. I hoped Winnie had only a single card of each suit. One more loss for me meant I'd lose the whole game.

Henry slept restlessly on the cot nearby, crammed between the bed and the door. He'd been drowsy and cranky throughout the afternoon. Mom and Viola had asked me to keep an eye on him while they sat for a bit downstairs with the Taylor women and Maggie Hollett. Surely they'd all earned a chance to sit and socialize for a space. Dad and the other men were out somewhere, still. Having a smoke and their own spot of gossip, I supposed.

The quiet voices rumbling downstairs were interrupted by a sudden boisterous clamor. I thought I heard Eddie's voice, so I wasn't surprised when my brother appeared at the door to our small room.

"They're making a good time down at the school," he said. "Mom said you could come along, Celia. And the Taylor girls too, if they want." He nodded at Dinah when he noticed her there.

"Not me?" Winnie said.

"Mom and Nan don't think it's a good idea, little sis," Eddie replied. "Too much noise for your tender head or some such." He softened his words with an easy grin.

"Oh, it's fine," Winnie said, smiling up at him. "I agree with them. My head does still pound something awful. I can't imagine adding music to that."

"That sounds fun," I said, standing up and patting my hair into place. "Will you be fine here, Winnie?"

She laughed softly. "They won't leave me alone for long."

I knew that was true. What with everyone worrying over her, Winnie was rarely ever alone these days. Besides, Henry was in the room with her, and they'd be checking on him shortly.

"So, are you coming or not, Celia?" Eddie was fair bouncing with excitement.

"Yes," I said, snapping a little at his impatience. "Just let me get my coat. And can you go ask Bessie if she'll come?"

He nodded and disappeared down the hallway. I looked back at Winnie, who was neatly stacking the cards. She glanced up at me and made a shooing gesture.

"Go have fun, CeeCee. I'm good, honest."

"See you in a bit, then."

Downstairs, there was a bustle of activity as us girls got ready to go down to the party. Mom and Viola were arguing quietly about whether they should leave Henry. Nan, overhearing them, put a stop to that with a stern glare.

"I can watch the boy, Addie. And keep an eye on Winnie. Go and have a spot of fun. We've had enough of turmoil and worry to do us for now, girl."

Mom still didn't look convinced, so I took her hand

and tugged her toward the door. "Come with us, Mom," I wheedled. "We all need the break."

She paused a moment longer, debating. "Oh, all right then. Thank you, Bea. It's a relief to know you're here to watch the kids."

We streamed out into the cold, tugging coats and hats into place. Mom, Viola, Dinah, Bessie, Mrs. Taylor, and I scurried down the path toward the schoolhouse. The night was very dark, the moon not yet risen. Voices carried through the still air, already loud and merry. I wasn't sure where Eddie had disappeared to.

Inside the school, folks were settled in small clumps on the benches and desks. A few kerosene lamps gave the room a dim glow. No one wanted to keep too many lamps lit when we didn't know how long we'd be without new fuel. Near the stove, old Uncle Isaiah had pulled out his fiddle and was checking the strings. I smiled. Leave it to the old sleveen to keep his fiddle safe in a disaster! Beside him, young John Rose held a tin whistle, the flat metal reflecting the flames from the closest lamp.

"Give us something lively, will ye, b'y?" called a voice from the corner. I couldn't make out who it was—an older man, from the sound of it.

"Aye, a jig for dancing," said someone else.

"'Tain't no room for dancing."

"We'll make it work. We all need a bit of a break."

I threaded my way through the gathered bodies and took up a seat on the floor by Uncle Isaiah's knee. Someone handed me an ugly stick. I could imagine where they'd found the broomstick, but wherever had they found the bits of metal? There were spoons and nails and other bits I didn't recognize. Likely someone had gone rummaging through wreckage to find all that. I shook the stick gently, and it jangled. It should add a pleasant bit of sound to the evening.

The old man gave me a gap-toothed grin and raised the fiddle to his shoulder, bow poised for movement and fingers ready to dance. Then the bow dropped to the strings, and the notes spilled out into the room—a lively, raucous tune that made my fingers and toes tap along. Around me, hands began to clap together, and I turned my head to see a pair of young men begin to dance.

The jig quickly turned into a competition. Each of the boys was trying to outdo the other. Feet flew in a flurry of movement, twirling and jumping and kicking out. When one finally stopped, breathing quickly, another stepped in to take his place. My brother Eddie stepped up with a smirk to take his turn. The musicians kept playing, one jig flowing into another. I shook the ugly stick and whooped along with the others, encouraging Eddie. Sweat beaded on the brows of both dancers. Eddie's hair was limp against his skull, and I could see a dark wet patch between his shoulder blades. Despite the obvious effort, he kept dancing, and his competitor was clearly tiring. Finally, they stopped and gave each other a bow.

Across the room I noticed Dinah watching with a dreamy expression. Interesting, that. Was she thinking of Eddie or the other fellow? Whatever would her family think if she said she wanted to go walking out with our Eddie? Personally, I couldn't imagine they'd be happy about it. Bessie, particularly. But I wasn't sure what their parents would say. That she could do better, like as not.

My thoughts were interrupted when my father came up and grabbed my hand. "Come on, Celia girl. Let's show them how it's done!"

I laughed and stood up, handing off the ugly stick. "I'm not sure I can outdo our Eddie, Dad."

"Nonsense."

He bowed slightly, and I curtsied. Then our feet were flying, moving to the music. My hair lifted with the speed of my twirls. Dad's eyes sparkled in the lamplight as he pulled me close, then spun me away. Sweat dampened my hairline and trickled down my back. My heart beat faster, and my breath strained in my chest. Around me, friends and neighbors clapped their encouragement. It was no longer a competition but a joyous celebration of the fact we were alive.

I finally wound to a stop, gulping the smoky air into my lungs. Dad pulled me close in a quick, rough hug. "That's my girl," he said softly into my ear. "You're a fine dancer. Someday all the lads will come calling and asking you to dance."

I giggled and blushed. "Like who?"

He looked at me and shrugged. "Oh, who knows. Perhaps you'll go off to Lamaline and meet some young fella with his own skiff, or even some as owns a store. Marrying up, eh?" He winked at me, his words mirroring my thoughts earlier about the Taylors and our Eddie.

I opened my mouth to reply. Before I could form any words, the schoolhouse door banged open and let in a large gust of frigid air and a billow of snow. When it cleared, everyone could see Nan standing there. The music trailed off. What had happened to bring her all the way down here by herself in the cold?

"Where's Addie?" Nan asked, her voice loud in the sudden silence. "She needs to come right away. It's Henry."

Mom, Viola, and I hurried back to the big house with Nan. They'd moved Henry down to the sitting room so that it was easier to move around. He'd grown much sicker since we'd left. Before, he'd mostly been sleeping soundly. Now he was tossing and turning, unaware of his surroundings. I was almost afraid to touch him. Mom did though, clicking her tongue against her teeth.

"He's burning up," she said brusquely. "Get me some cool water and fresh clothes, will you Celia? Viola...fetch me a cup of water. One of those aspirin tablets might help with the fever."

Cool water? There wasn't much water, but plenty of snow. And wouldn't cold be better than cool if he was fevered? I dashed outside and scooped up a double handful of clean, heavy snow. It was awkward, but after a few moments struggle with the door, I was inside with the precious load of snow and back at Henry's side.

Mom looked up at me. I must have looked quite the sight because she grinned despite the seriousness of the situation.

"Cool water, Celia. Not frozen." She pointed toward the kitchen. "Find yourself a pot, girl, and set that to melting. It's no good to us like that."

"But wouldn't it be better? Cool him off faster?"

"No, dear girl. You can cause shock that way. Go and set it to melt, now."

"Oh." I deflated. The snow in my hands was already beginning to melt, soaking into my mittens. I trudged into the kitchen. Nan was there fussing at the stove. She took one look at me and understood the situation.

"Here, Celia," she said, pulling the wash cauldron from under the sink. "Dump that in and take your mother some water from that bucket there. We've been keeping it ready for whatever comes."

"It's not warm, is it?" I asked, brushing snow from my mittens. "Mom said she needed cool water."

"No, it's not been melted long."

"That'll do. Have we clean clothes?"

"Clean? Or did she say sterile?"

I didn't know that word, so I was sure Mom hadn't used it. I would have asked about it. "Just clean."

"Take something from the basket of clothes we collected, child. It's by the window."

"Yes, I saw it. Anything?"

She nodded, her silvered hair impeccably in place despite the trials of the last few days. "I think it doesn't much matter."

"True. Thank you."

Back in the sitting room, Mom and Viola were examining Henry's leg. I could mostly make out their expressions in the shadows—worried. It must be as bad as I thought. Maybe even worse! I lugged the half-full bucket over to them and set it down with a thump. Viola glanced at me. "That was quick," she said.

"Nan had some ready. The snow I brought in is melting now. She told me to get something out of the clothing basket, so long as you don't need them...what did she say...sterile?"

"No, that'll do nicely. We just need something to help cool Henry down. On his forehead, his chest."

That made sense. I pulled the pile of clothes into the lamplight near Henry's cot and started rummaging through it. Would wool do, or was cotton, like the lighter dresses, better? I held up a set of pants and a dress and quirked an eyebrow at my mother. She was holding Henry's wrist between her fingers, brow creased with concentration. Was she counting? Whatever for?

I waggled the cloth again and drew Viola's attention. "The dress, I think," she said, tapping her chin. "Let's get it torn into strips and soaking in the water. We'll want the cloth wet, but not sogged."

Nan came in then with a cup of steaming liquid. I glanced up at her, but she didn't say anything. Instead, she joined Mom by Henry's bedside.

We worked in silence, loosening the seams to reveal unfinished edges that were easier to tear. Viola smoothly tore even strips. I watched and tried to imitate her, but my pieces ended up rough and uneven. My sister noticed and smiled with encouragement. "It takes a practiced hand to get it neat. Doesn't matter though, it'll work regardless. All's we need is smaller pieces, see."

Where had she learned all this about nursing? I imagined she must have taken care of the children at the big house in Lamaline when they were sick, but she'd never once told me about it. She'd picked up some useful skills for sure. One day it was likely to be me learning new things.

I didn't have a chance to ask her any of the questions I had, though. I dropped my uneven strips of cloth into the bucket and stretched my aching back. The kitchen door banged open then, and the Taylor kids came in like a gaggle of geese. Mom glared at them, and they quieted down.

"Can't you see this is a sickroom just now?" she hissed at them from between her teeth.

"Sorry, Mrs. Matthews," Clancy whispered before tiptoeing up the stairs.

Bessie looked down her nose at us and didn't say a word before she left. Dinah gave an apologetic shrug and slowly followed her siblings upstairs. Ollie, one of Henry's closest friends, stopped for a moment longer to watch.

"Is he going to be all right?"

Viola sighed, but Mom spared Ollie a sympathetic glance. "I think so," she said. "He's a strong boy. We just need to keep him cool for now."

Ollie didn't say anything. He just stood awkwardly at the bottom of the stairs.

"Get on with you, rascal," Viola said. "There's nothing you can do just now."

"When he wakes…well, just tell him I can't wait to get out jigging with him again."

No one answered. After a moment, Ollie went up the stairs too. I wondered if they were all going to bed. Was Winnie sleeping? Did she know how sick our Henry was? Surely she'd have heard the hubbub as they moved him.

"Get another cloth, will you CeeCee?" Viola said quietly. "This one's near dry already."

We continued on, helping to cool Henry's flushed skin with damp cloths. He was still restless, mumbling words we couldn't hear or make sense of. Mom and Viola looked worried. No one was talking, though, so I couldn't be sure how concerned they really were. After a while, Mom stretched her arms overhead with a sigh. I could hear her joints popping. "I'm going to find some water," she said. "I need a drink, and we'd best get some into Henry too. He's like to be parched with how hot he's running."

"There's some fresh snow-melt in the kitchen," I said. "'Course it's in the washtub, so…maybe not the best for drinking."

Mom grimaced. "It's all right. I'll get some fresh snow in a pot," she said. "We can use the other for washing up."

She and Nan headed into the kitchen and left us kids in the semidarkness.

Henry had settled some, so I perched on the rocking chair. Viola fluttered around the room. From the kitchen we heard quiet conversation—Mom, Dad, Nan, Mrs. Taylor. I couldn't tell what time it was—there was no moonlight, and outside was full dark. How long had we been here caring for my brother? It felt late. The whole house was still, and there was no sound or movement outside either. I couldn't hear any more music, not even the slightest bit. Was the party done, then? Was everyone else in town abed?

"Celia?" Viola said quietly as she stopped walking. I looked up at her. "Get some sleep. I've got Henry for now. I'll wake you in a bit if I need you."

"You sure?"

She nodded. "Grab a blanket or something. You want to curl up in the corner or go upstairs and climb in with Winnie?"

"Here's fine. I'm some tired, Vi. Thanks."

"You're welcome, CeeCee."

I bundled my coat into a makeshift pillow and pulled a knitted blanket out of the chest by the door, then I curled up in a dark corner of the room. The rocking chair creaked as Viola settled into it. Mom walked softly back into the room, her footsteps light on the squeaky floorboards. I closed my eyes. Sleep was winning out over my desire to stay awake and help. As I drifted off, I heard small sounds around me—the thunk of a cup being set down, quiet steps, the soft whoosh of the lamp as it was put out. My family was here; I was warm and safe.

Finally, I fell deeply asleep.

Chapter 11
THE DARKEST HOUR

Friday, November 22, 2:00 p.m.

The duck stew was the last we had of any decent food. Over the next day, things grew steadily worse. A fox killed several of the chickens so we had no more eggs, and we ate the last of the vegetables from the Taylors' shed. Eddie had no more luck finding ducks. The fish in the bay had all but disappeared. My stomach started to hurt from being so hungry, but I knew better than to complain. Clancy whined on and off until his mother lost her head and shouted at him. Bessie looked ready to deck him. When he burst into tears and ran outside,

Dinah was the only one who had enough sympathy left to follow him.

For myself, I was just grateful to have a break from his whinging.

Nan and Gran Taylor sat close to the stove talking in low voices. Surprisingly, they seemed to be getting along fine. With how strong and independent they both were, I couldn't help but be surprised by that. I curled myself small and settled in to listen.

"…Nothing left of the preserves?" Nan asked.

"Just a bit of cucumber pickle," Gran Taylor replied, making a face. "Not enough to get by on."

"Something for the lad, maybe?"

"Yes, I suppose. Get him to shut his trap for a bit."

Nan nodded. "I hear it's worse down at the school. A few babes in arms there who can't help but wail from hunger."

"Pickle's no good for the ones that young," Gran Taylor said, shaking her head.

All the talk about food just reminded me of my growling tummy. That was no good. Soon I'd be whining just as much as Clancy, and nobody needed that. I stood up and stretched. Maybe Mom needed some help with Henry. Or maybe Winnie and Dinah were interested in a game of cards.

I tiptoed into the sitting room. No need to wake

Henry if he was resting, after all. Mom leaned back in the rocking chair, snoring softly. Viola sat close to the fire keeping an eye on Henry. I paused to check on him too.

"He's restless," Viola whispered as I came near. "Muttering nonsense. And still so hot and feverish." She smoothed a freshly dampened cloth over his forehead as she spoke. His dark hair was wet with sweat, his face flushed bright pink. Was it possible he wouldn't recover? I tried to imagine a world without Henry around to bug me. It didn't seem possible. Thinking about it made my stomach dip like I was standing on the edge of a cliff. I hadn't known baby Ruthie well, so losing her hadn't hurt me near as much as I figured losing Henry would. I hesitated. Should I ask for details? I doubted Viola could tell me anything new.

"Where's the men?" I asked, switching subjects. Maybe that would stop me from thinking about worst-case situations.

"Out," she said, gesturing vaguely. "Looking to patch up a dory or two, I think. Now the storm's stopped, they're making plans to get out looking for help. You and Henry showed them it has to be by sea."

"Can't say if that's brave or foolish," I muttered.

"Now you sound just like Mom!"

I chuckled ruefully. "Is that a good thing?"

There was a long pause. "It's a grown-up thing," she said finally.

I looked down, pleating my skirt with my fingers. How strange for her to call me grown up. I had no idea how to respond. I surely didn't feel all that grown up. I felt tired, cold, scared. My stomach was both full of flutters and aching with hunger. My mind was full of silly ideas and loads of worries, all crashing around and making my head spin. I didn't know what to do to help Henry. Infections were one thing I knew nothing about. I worried about Mom and Viola and Winnie. They were all so tired and worn, and surely as hungry as I was. I fretted over Dad, Eddie, and Uncle Bert. What risks would they take to look after us? I tried to imagine any one of them gone, and my stomach dipped and dived with worry.

The door from the kitchen banged open. Bessie stormed into the sitting room. "That privy is disgusting!" she exclaimed at the top of her lungs, completely interrupting my thoughts. "Someone ought to dig us a new one." Her eyes swept over Viola, Henry, and I. "Where's that lout of a brother of yours? He'd be a dab hand at digging holes, I imagine."

My blood boiled and heat rushed through my body. How dare she speak to us that way? I found myself on my feet, hands balled into fists at my side. Viola was standing too. I wasn't sure if she meant to grab hold of me or take a swing at Bessie. It didn't matter. I took a step toward Bessie and scowled.

"Can't you see Henry's resting?" Viola said, in her best impression of Mom's serious tone.

Bessie flicked her eyes over my brother's sleeping form and sighed loudly. "My Gran says he's getting worse," she said, dismissing any of our concerns. "Said the infection's like to cost him the leg if not more."

"You take that back, Bessie Taylor!" I cried, crossing the room in three steps and grabbing hold of her collar. Nose to nose, we both narrowed our eyes. My face felt hot, and the pressure was building up inside me like a kettle about to boil. No way was she right. She and her meddling grandmother were both just being nasty.

"Why?" she hissed. "It's only the truth."

"What does your grandmother know about nursing anyway?" I snarled back. "She's never had to worry about that a day in her life. Always someone else's job."

Bessie shrieked in my ear and pushed me backward. I had such a grip on her dress that she came tumbling down with me. We landed in a heap on the floor, each of us grabbing for whatever we could reach. My hand connected with her ear, and she had hold of my hair. We wrestled and tussled, rolling around on the neatly swept floorboards until we came right up against the wall. I pulled hard on her ear, and she let go of my hair to scratch my face. We both growled.

There were raised voices around me but I couldn't make any sense of what they were saying. I grabbed Bessie's hand and leaned in to bite her fingers. My teeth never connected. Instead, I found myself dangling above the ground in the strong grip of my father. "I think that's enough, girl," he said mildly as I struggled to get loose.

Across the room, my mother's expression was not nearly as mild. She stood by the rocking chair, her face stony serious. My heart dropped, and my stomach fluttered just looking at her. "Give her here, George," she said.

Dad set me on my feet and steered me over to my mother. I stood silently in front of her, looking at my feet. How had I let Bessie needle me so much? Mom and Henry had both been sleeping. Our fight had woken Mom from her much-needed rest. And Viola had just been saying how grown up I was! A rush of heat spread through my body, reddening my cheeks. We'd been squabbling like a pair of right scoundrels. It wasn't like me. Henry was the one to use his fists to solve problems, not me.

"Everyone's feeling the strain, Addie," Dad said calmly. He stayed clear of Mom as he spoke, though. He must not be trusting her temper either.

"Not everyone's acting like a wild animal," Mom replied, biting each word short. "Celia, get yourself upstairs and stay there till we call for you. As for you, Bessie…."

"She can go and clean the privy," said Gran Taylor firmly from the kitchen doorway. "Seeing as that started this whole mess."

Bessie began to protest. As much as part of me wanted to stay and listen, that was likely to get me in more trouble. No need to draw more of Gran Taylor's temper. I trudged up the stairs and into the room I shared with Winnie. My sister gave me a startled look as I grabbed a pillow to stifle my giggles. It really wouldn't do to have my parents hear me laughing. They'd likely decide I needed hard labor too. I was a little surprised that Gran Taylor had let me get away with simple banishment upstairs.

Once I stopped laughing, I explained the whole situation to Winnie. She listened quietly, eyes growing rounder and rounder as I described the tussle. By the time I got to Bessie's punishment, Winnie was giggling too.

"Oh, I can just picture her face," she wheezed. "She must have been right livid."

"Yes, I suppose. But so was everyone else—Mom, Nan, Gran Taylor…."

"Not Dad, from what you said."

"No," I said slowly. "No, he didn't seem angry at all. Isn't that strange?"

Winnie shook her head carefully. I wondered how bad the headache was. "You don't give him enough credit," she said. "Dad knows how Bessie is. And he gets people. He knows what you've been feeling, what all of us have been feeling. He won't be blaming you, CeeCee."

I wasn't sure. It certainly felt like part of the blame fell on me. No matter how mean or snooty Bessie got, wasn't it up to me to not let her get to me like that? I opened my mouth to say just that, but Winnie's knowing look stopped me short.

"No one's going to blame you, Celia," she said with gentle force.

"You don't?"

"'Course not," she said with a giggle. "Bessie got what was coming and not a bit more."

How odd, both of my sisters offering wisdom on the same day. Did that mean we were all growing up? I pushed that thought aside for later. Right now I didn't have the energy to examine it further. Instead, I grinned at Winnie. Time to be just a kid again.

"Do you know where the cards are?"

Chapter 12
THE S.S. MEIGLE

Saturday, November 23, 12:30 p.m.

"Can we eat pine needles? Or bark?" I asked wistfully as I sat keeping watch over Henry. He slipped in and out of sleep, mumbling nonsense. He was burning hot despite our efforts to cool him, and I'd seen the worry on Mom's face over it.

"Are you a deer?" Viola replied tartly. "They're the only creature I know of as can eat pine."

"Maybe a bear," Dinah chimed in. She shuddered slightly.

The mention of the bear brought me back to those

terrible moments in the shed, and I was sure she felt the same way. My heart pounded heavily, and my palms were slippery with sweat. I knew we were safe, that there was no bear, but my body seemed to disagree.

"I need to move a bit. You good for watching Henry?"

Viola grunted but waved me on. "Go ahead. I'll take a walk later on."

Dinah rose to go with me. "I need some fresh air myself."

We pulled on coats and boots and headed out into the sunshine. Drawn as ever to the sights along the beach, I turned toward the bay. As we drew closer, something different caught my attention. I stopped and shaded my eyes.

"What is it?" Dinah asked, peering out to sea.

"Not sure yet."

We walked further along the path, closer to the government wharf. I kept my eyes on the speck I thought I'd seen.

"Is that a ship?" I said, after staring for a few more minutes.

Dinah stretched up on her toes as if to get a better look. "Might be," she said doubtfully.

A few of the boys joined us. Everyone was tense, not daring to hope for anything. No one spoke more than a few muttered words here and there. The sun, bright overhead, cast shadows and reflections on the choppy water of the bay and the larger ocean beyond.

"That is a ship," Dinah said, barely breathing.

"A big one," Ollie agreed, grabbing her arm to pull himself up taller.

"Like the coastal boat?" asked little Clancy.

I nodded. It was a ship. Finally.

Excitement threatened to burst out of my chest, and my whole body suddenly felt lighter. A ship! Surely we were saved. There would be news, supplies. Medicine for Henry and more aspirin for Winnie. There had to be.

More people began to gather as word spread. Viola appeared, pulling several shawls tight around her body. We stood near the wharf and the ruins of our home. The beach and flat spaces were still littered with broken boards, the whole of it covered in drifts of snow. The tracks where folks had walked here and there, searching through the wreckage, stood out clear against the white. The Hollett house still floated in the bay, and beyond it loomed the slowly advancing prow of the ship.

"I can see someone on deck," Viola exclaimed.

"Looks like they're getting the boat ready," Eddie said. "Just as well as there's no dock to moor at."

"Aye, and they can see that, ye great lout." Uncle

Bert appeared just in time to chime in on the conversation. He punched Eddie in the shoulder to show he was joking.

We watched, huddled together for warmth, as the people on board lowered the small boat to the water. It was hard to see details, but it looked full of people. The dory disappeared briefly, blocked from view by floating debris, then reappeared as they rowed closer. A few of the men moved toward the shoreline to meet them.

It wasn't long before the boat pulled ashore. The men helped the newcomers clamber onto the rocky beach. Boomer padded up to Dad, tail wagging, and barked. Just like him to stop by to say hello.

A short, round-faced man stepped forward, his gaze sweeping the wreckage of the town. He was dressed neatly in a dapper city suit that looked very much out of place on our beach. Who was he? Some big-shot politician most like. "What's your situation?" he asked, looking around at the gathered villagers.

"Six dead," old Jack Taylor replied. "Most of the houses gone, as ye can see. Coal and kerosene running out. All the flakes and stored cod gone. Food's run out, near enough."

"Injuries?" the newcomer inquired.

"Aye, a few. Up at the big house yonder—the one as belongs to the storekeep. My daughter had a good bump to the head, my youngest son a nasty cut that's festering," Dad said.

"Any signs of contagious disease?" the man asked. "Coughs, vomiting, rashes, or the like?"

The villagers frowned, shuffling feet and shaking their heads. "No," Jack said. "None of that, thanks be to God."

"All right." The stranger turned back to his group of followers. "Signal for medical, right lads? And let's see to getting some hot food for these folks too. We'll get onto other supplies in a jiffy."

A wave of relief washed through me. Help had arrived! Medicine and food at the very least, which we were in dire need of. Nothing else really mattered. Medicine! Surely now we could really help Henry, and perhaps there was more to be done for Winnie too. I felt lighter, as if I could dance a jig again like I had with Dad a few days before. The weight lifted from my shoulders.

Torn between wanting to run back up to the house to share the good news with Mom or stay and watch the activity, I turned toward my sister. Viola was shivering, arms wrapped close around her. "You go on back," I said. "Tell Mom what's happened and get yourself warm again."

She nodded, clamping shut her teeth to keep them from chattering. "Be sure to come back with the medicine," she said curtly. "I'm sure Mom will need help still."

"Yes, I will." For a moment I bristled at her tone, but I quickly realized it was mostly because she was shivering so hard. And maybe out of worry or excitement. She and some of the other villagers headed back to the relative warmth of inside, feet slipping on the snowy path. Only a few of us had boots worth their leather, and only a few more had escaped the water with their coats and mitts. More of the men had, to be sure—those who had been out and about the evening of the disaster. But us women? Not as much. In a way, it was lucky I'd gone out looking for Boomer and had been dressed for the cold.

Many of the children stayed to watch the unloading of supplies. Eddie and Uncle Bert left to join the men down at the beach, adding their strong arms and backs to the efforts of pulling the dories ashore and unloading crates and bundles from them. I brushed some snow off a flat boulder and settled down on its cold surface to observe the goings-on. It was nice to be out in the crisp air. Overhead, the sky was partly gray, but there were none of the heavy, dark clouds that promised more snow. I took a few deep breaths of the cold, salty air.

Boomer ran around among the men on the beach for a while, his thick tail wagging everywhere he went.

Eventually he trotted over to me and sat down. I reached out to scratch his ears. He let out a soft moan of delight and leaned into my hand.

After a while, Dinah joined me on my rocky perch. She, like Viola, was bundled in several layers of sweaters and shawls. One of them looked like Nan's. Her face was pink with cold and excitement. She leaned against me. "I can't believe it!" she said breathlessly. "I heard they've been all up and down the coast, dropping off medicine and food. Seems that wave hit near the whole shore, from Port au Bras 'round to Point May."

"Where'd you hear that?" I asked, shifting a bit on the hard surface. We'd not been apart that much. How had she heard more news than me?

Dinah blushed pinker. "The menfolk," she stammered, looking down at her hands.

"Oh?" I said. Her reaction was curious. Whyever was she blushing over that?

"Your brother Eddie said so to my father. He'd heard it from a sailor on the boat."

Well, now. That cleared up my question from the kitchen party the other night. Sweet on Eddie, was she? I wondered if he knew.

I decided not to mention it. Instead, I asked one of my many other questions. "Where'd she come from?"

"The ship? All the way from St. John's, they said."

"How'd they find out what happened?"

Dinah shrugged. "Nobody told me, yet. I'm guessing we'll hear eventually. When they decide to include us kids."

That was frustrating, considering how much we'd been doing to help. I jumped to my feet. "I'm not going to wait for that," I declared, dusting snow off my skirt. "If I go ask, they'll tell me. Something, at least." I looked back at Dinah. "You coming?"

She stared at me, shocked. "But they're busy!" she exclaimed. "There's so much going on down there."

"You afraid to go talk to my brother?"

That brought her to her feet, eyes full of fire. "No, I'm not afraid of anything."

"Yeah? Then why are you stalling? Let's go ask."

This time I didn't look back. My boots slipped on the path down to the beach, but I didn't lose my balance or stumble. I found Eddie leaning on a crate near the shore, taking a drag on a cigarette. He waved, sending a circle of smoke up into the sky.

"Hey, little sis," he said. "What're you up to?"

"Waiting for medicine," I replied.

"Waiting for the nurse, you mean," he countered. "There's one aboard. She's coming in on the next dory."

"That's good, we need some help with Henry."

Eddie nodded. "Aye, that we do." He took another long drag on the cigarette.

"When did you start smoking?" I asked, stepping out of the way as he blew smoke toward me.

"On the schooner," he replied with a shrug. "Not always work to do when you're going in or out."

"Oh." I paused and looked over my shoulder. Dinah was hovering but not coming too close. "Did you hear anything about how the government found out about all this?" I waved vaguely at the debris-strewn shoreline.

"Not much. Just that the S.S. *Portia* pulled into Burin on her regular route and saw all that'd happened there. She had a radio aboard. Sent a message straight away."

Dinah edged closer. "Did they say how bad it is, down Burin way?"

"Not so much. Just that the *Meigle* here is near out of supplies and may take a jaunt over to the French islands to get some more."

My stomach grumbled and gurgled. How long had it been since that duck stew? "They mentioned food. Any sign of it yet?"

"Always thinking of your stomach, eh?" Eddie said with a laugh. "I swear you're worse than Henry!"

I stuck my tongue out at him. "And you're *not* hungry?"

"Didn't say that," he said, blowing smoke at me. "You're the one who brought up the idea of food though."

"I'm hungry too," Dinah said with a sigh. "Can we stop talking about it?"

"Sure thing," Eddie said. "Now, little ladies, clear out. Next boat's coming in." He dropped the cigarette and rubbed it into the snow with one booted foot.

We backed up a ways to watch. The prow of the dory dipped and rose with the waves as the oarsmen rowed toward the shore. I could just make out the starched white cap of the nurse amid the darker colors of the men. The boat appeared to be loaded with more crates. I wondered which of them held the promised medicine. Would anything they'd brought be of help? It had to be. We'd waited so long.

Shortly, the dory came ashore, and the young men got busy unloading it. My father walked toward us, the nurse scurrying along beside him. "We haven't anything left by way of medical supplies," Dad said as they passed by. "There's been no illness, but injuries—yes, injuries we've had."

The nurse nodded, her pale-brown curls bobbing under the rim of her cap. "I'll have a look, and the lads will bring up supplies." Her voice was crisp but gentle. She wasn't an islander though—had she come from England? I didn't recognize her accent except that it marked her as from away.

I was torn. On the one hand, there was a great deal of activity down by the shore, and it was nice to be outside in the fresh air. On the other hand, the best way to find out what was going on at the house was to be there. And I really did want to know if this angel in white could help either Winnie or Henry. Plus, I'd as much as promised Viola I'd come back. With one last look over my shoulder, I followed Dad.

Chapter 13
NURSE WILCOX

Saturday, 2:00 p.m.

Up at the Taylor house there was a renewed sense of energy and purpose. Viola met us at the door, fluttering and pink in the face. The Taylors themselves bustled about, but Nan shooed them out of the sitting room so we'd have some space for the nurse to work. Winnie sat in a chair by the fire, blanket tucked around her. Mom paced between the window and the stairs.

Viola grabbed my arm. "Is there medicine? Does she think she'll be able to do something for Henry?"

"I don't know, Vi. Hang 'er down and we'll find out from the folks that know!"

The nurse pulled off her coat and hung it on one of the hooks by the door. Then, she smoothed her neat starched uniform and smiled at my mother. "Hello. I'm Eliza Wilcox. Let's have a look, shall we?"

Mom bobbed her head. "Addie Matthews. This here's my son, Henry. He's fevered from a bad cut on his leg. We've not been able to do much save keep the fever from getting too hot."

Eliza pulled back the covers. Her expression was intent as she leaned in close to examine the dressing. She wrinkled her nose. "Aye, I can smell it festering. How'd he get hurt?"

Mom gestured to me. "My daughter Celia was with him. What do you remember, my girl?"

I sidled closer, feeling suddenly shy. It wasn't often we met someone completely new here in Taylor's Bay. I took a breath. "He slipped a few days ago when we were out looking for help. We thought maybe a nail or broken board did it. We did meet a nurse that day, come down from Lamaline. She helped us patch him up and left us a few aspirin, but she couldn't stay."

"Aspirin's gone," Mom said quietly. "Winnie's needed it for her head, although I gave a couple to Henry to help with the fever too."

"Hmm," Eliza murmured, unraveling the strips of cloth we'd used as a bandage. Underneath, Henry's leg was red and swollen around the pine-sap dressing. Streaks of red ran up his thigh away from the cut. "Looks like the infection's getting into his blood. I've some Cartel-Dakin solution that might help. We'll have to remove this dressing, though."

"What's that?" Mom asked.

"It's a liquid that helps kill infection when applied to a wound. We'll need to get it inside, though, where the infection is. Just putting it on the outside won't do anything. Maybe a needle would do it, but I'd rather be sure."

"Sounds simple enough," Mom said.

"Depends on how well closed the cut is," the nurse replied. "We might have to cut it open again."

Viola blanched. I agreed—that did not sound like it would be much fun for anyone. I felt a bit woozy at the thought and couldn't imagine how much that would hurt Henry.

"Once we've got the wound open to the air, I'll be able to show you how to treat it properly. Then you'll be good to go on your own."

"You're not able to stay?" Viola blurted.

"No, sadly, I must go on with the *Meigle*. We've many more stops to make."

My stomach dropped. "But what if we need more help? What if Henry doesn't get better, or someone else gets hurt?" The tone of my voice startled everyone, even me. Mom gave me a serious look, but it was tinged with exhaustion and worry. Viola was biting her lip. Winnie looked on silently, sipping at a cup of water. I would lay a wager we were all thinking the same thing.

Eliza took a moment to cover Henry with the blanket before answering. "The *Meigle* hasn't space to take anyone new aboard," she said slowly. "Now that we've seen the extent of things, we'll contact St. John's. Surely they'll be sending other ships to help."

There was an awkward silence. I paced restlessly, not sure what to do or say. When Eliza spoke again, this time to Winnie, I hurried close to hear what she had to say.

"I hear you had a blow to the head, child," she said softly. "Has your head been sore much? Dizzy? Sick to the stomach?"

Winnie nodded at each question. "Yes," she said in a very small voice. "All of that. I've had some aspirin, but I still have a headache, miss."

"Come close to the window, please. Let me take a good look."

Winnie stood up, wobbling slightly. She limped toward the window on her twisted leg. The blanket trailed behind her. The nurse's expression changed slightly as she followed. I bristled in indignation. No one stared at my sister! Her limp was just a part of her—not a fault or a weakness.

"Have you always had the limp, child, or is that new?"

Winnie steadied herself against the table. "Oh, that's always been the way of it," she replied. "My foot just turns in, you see." She sat down again and arranged the blanket around herself.

"I can have a look after, see if there's anything to be done," Eliza said.

My mother settled beside Winnie. "It's fine," she said. "It's just the way things are."

Eliza looked from Mom to Winnie to me and back again. "If you think that's right," she said at last. "Now, young lady. Let me have a look at you." She placed her hands on Winnie's head, feeling around the back and top of her skull. Her expression was still and focused. I wondered what she was thinking. Could she feel something that would explain Winnie's headache or the way she'd been out of consciousness for so long? My questions remained unanswered, however, as Eliza moved her hands to cup Winnie's chin and lifted her head up slightly. My sister winced. I knew it was her pounding head and nearly spoke up. The nurse noticed, however, and made her movements even more gentle. She peered into Winnie's eyes, carefully turning my sister's head this way and that.

"Follow my finger," Eliza said at last, holding up one hand. "Try not to move your head, though. Just your eyes."

Winnie did as instructed. I could tell it took an effort not to move her head, though. What did that mean?

"Good job, child. Now, can you tell me what happened? Did you fall, or did something fall on you?"

My sister frowned. "That's part of the trouble, see. I really don't remember." She plucked at the blanket in her lap. "I remember the shaking. We were making dinner—special, for Celia's birthday. Then we went outside. I think we were going to the store? I remember something about the telephone. And then, I don't know. It's all fuzzy and broken into bits and pieces. Almost like a dream." She paused again, then continued slowly. "I know there was a lot of shouting, a lot of noise. But that's all."

"That's all right, child. It's normal to have trouble remembering after an injury to your head." Eliza looked up at Mom. "Were there any cuts or bleeding?"

"No, nothing like that. We were terrible surprised when she wouldn't wake, on account of that."

"I understand. The doctors say that you can injure your brain, inside the skull, even when there's no wound on the outside."

"Oh?" Mom said, a hundred questions in the one word.

"So they say," Eliza replied with a shrug. "I think our patient here needs some gentle activity, as much as she can tolerate. I've some more aspirin tablets to help with the pain as well. Likely enough to help young Henry too. It may give him more strength to fight the infection."

"Yes, of course. We always kept some at the house, before." Her expression grew somber. I understood the feeling. I couldn't help thinking about how it was all gone. I was sure all of us had those thoughts in passing.

Eliza caught the mood too. She was quiet for a moment, kneeling in front of Winnie. Eventually she stood up, her movements brisk and purposeful. "Let's have the men bring up the medical crates. I'll show you how to use the Carrel-Dakin solution. Celia, girl. Please go down to the boats and ask for the medical crates to be brought up, will you?"

I bristled at her tone. *Girl,* from this come-from-away? It was one thing if my parents called me that—I was *their* girl, their daughter. But I was not Eliza Wilcox's daughter. Besides, I wanted to stay and hear more of what she had to say.

"Go on, Celia," Mom said firmly. "Be a help to us all."

I opened my mouth to protest, then shut it again before saying anything. I was the natural choice. Mom and Viola should stay, as they'd been nursing everyone the most. Henry, clearly, couldn't go anywhere. And Winnie wasn't up for the task yet either. I doubted the trek down to the boats was the type of gentle exercise Eliza had in mind for her.

"Yes, Mom," I said, going to grab my coat and mitts.

Chapter 14
DECISIONS

Saturday, midnight

Voices from the sitting room woke me in the deep of night. There was something to the quality of those voices that stoked my curiosity. I got up carefully, so as not to wake my sisters, and crept to the top of the stairs.

"I'm not going anywhere," said a rough male voice I didn't recognize.

"That's your right," replied my father. "For myself? I have two children injured, no house, no boat. I have to think of them."

"Houses we can build," said a third voice. A

woman's. Was it Mrs. Taylor? "We've scraps and fresh lumber from the *Meigle*. This is my home, George. I say we stay."

"Stay if you will," my father said quietly. "I figure I must go. Burin, St. John's—wherever we must go to get help for my kids."

"Each of us must decide for ourself," said Nan, her voice strong. "I'll stay so long as Bert does. George must choose for himself, though. He's got his own family to think of beyond me."

There was a swell of sound as voices rose, arguing back and forth. I sat quiet as a mouse on the top step. Leave Taylor's Bay? All of us? I'd imagined leaving, someday—to go into service somewhere like Viola or to marry and start my own family. But now? It didn't seem possible. This was our home, our family's place in the world. All of our memories were here. The graves of our family, too. Great-Nan, PopPop, baby Ruthie. The familiar bay, the pond, the gnarly pine trees. How could we leave all of that behind? We'd never come back if we left like that. It wouldn't be like Viola going off to Lamaline. There would be no house, no family here to come back to. My stomach twisted just thinking about it.

My eyes stung—there was no house to stay in anyway. How could we stay? But how could we go? Both options felt horribly wrong. Warm, salty tears slid down my cheeks, and I rubbed them away. Crying was no use. It wouldn't help me or anyone else. My family needed me to be strong so I could help take care of Winnie and Henry. If we stayed to rebuild, there would be a lot of work to do. If we left for elsewhere, we'd have a lot to do setting up a new house. Either way, they'd need me. I swallowed the lump in my throat and stood up.

When I turned around, Viola was standing there. She looked at me solemnly.

"Do you think we'll go, then?" she said in a quiet voice. I could tell she was staying quiet so we didn't wake anyone. Her face was hidden by shadows, but I knew she was worried.

"I don't know. I don't want to."

Viola nodded. "Yes, I understand that. But what of the kids?"

I shrugged, a small helpless gesture. "There's not a good choice, is there?"

"No," she agreed. "Come on back to bed, CeeCee. We'll not be making the decision, and I don't think they'll decide anything tonight."

I didn't feel sleepy, but Viola was right. No sense sitting here and getting colder when there was a warm bed to curl up in. Any decisions were not ours to make. We'd hear about it in the morning if Mom and Dad had decided by then. We went back into the room together.

Viola pulled back the covers. "You go ahead," she whispered. "Sharing with Winnie's warmer, and you've been out longer."

"Might be restless," I whispered back.

She shrugged and climbed in. I curled up on the blankets on the floor and burrowed in. For a while, I lay awake in the darkness, listening to my sisters breathing. I couldn't hear any more voices from downstairs—did that mean everyone was gone to their beds? Or just that the conversation had quieted? Hard to say. Eventually my body relaxed into sleep.

When I woke in the morning, I was alone in the room. I could hear people downstairs—voices rising and falling, the low clatter of dishes. I sniffed the air. Was that breakfast? Hot butter, warm biscuits. Definitely breakfast. I untangled myself from the blankets and pulled on my fresh dress, courtesy of the folks in St. John's, then padded down the stairs in my stocking feet.

"Morning, sleepyhead," Winnie said cheerfully. She was settled in a chair by the stove, dressed neatly in a new dress. Her hair was brushed and gleaming chestnut in the morning light. I was glad to see her looking better.

"Morning," I replied. My stomach rumbled loudly.

"Here, girl," Mom said, handing me a plate with a warm buttered biscuit and a scoop of eggs on it. "Sit yourself down and eat. Then we've work to do."

I looked up at my mother. What work did she mean? Something different than all we'd been doing lately? Mom noticed my expression and gave me a warning frown. "Eat, Celia. We'll talk in a bit."

I bit into the biscuit—Nan's cooking, I could tell. It was like a little bite of heaven. The soft butter melted in my mouth, the biscuit itself falling apart. The bite of egg was equally divine, perfectly soft. My stomach gurgled as the food slid into it. I could not remember any food ever tasting this good. Was it only because I'd never been this hungry before? It didn't really matter. I tried to eat slowly, but it took a great effort. I wanted to devour every morsel as quickly as possible and find out what Mom had to say.

While I was eating, a few other folks wandered into the kitchen—Eddie, Uncle Bert, and the Taylor boys. Each of them snagged a fresh biscuit from the plate on the table and bit into it as he settled. My uncle leaned against the wall while Eddie sat on the floor in front of Winnie. The Taylor boys vanished into the sitting room. Viola appeared at my side, taking my plate over to the washtub.

"How's the womenfolk?" Eddie said, looking around at us.

"Well enough," Viola replied from the sink. Mom nodded, stirring eggs at the stove.

"And Henry?" Eddie asked.

"Getting better, I think. Only time will tell." Mom's voice was tired and strained.

"What of the medicine they left?"

"It's helping," Mom said firmly. "But it needs time to work."

Dad came in just then, pulling the door shut behind him with a thump. Everyone looked over at him with an air of expectation. Would we be hearing a decision? What were our parents planning? Did they know we'd overheard their conversation last night? He pulled up a chair beside Winnie and gave Mom a tired smile. "Might I be having some of those eggs, Addie?" he asked.

Wordlessly, Mom made him up a plate. There were more eggs on it than I'd gotten, but I supposed that was fair. He was bigger, after all. Used more energy or something. My stomach grumbled a bit though, still hungry. Dad grinned at me and nudged the plate of biscuits closer. "Have something to eat, girl."

"Oh, I've already eaten," I replied. It was enough

for now, surely. I didn't want to take more than my fair share.

"It's fine, Celia. Have another." Dad picked up one of the cooling biscuits and bit into it. "No one ought to be hungry now that we've the relief supplies from the *Meigle*."

I waited a moment, fiddling with my skirt, before reaching out to take another biscuit. Part of me expected someone to protest, but I knew that was silly. Dad had said it was fine so surely it must be. Still, there was a small guilty voice in the back of my head wondering if someone else might need it more than me. I couldn't fathom who, though.

Viola finished her washing up and came to stand beside me. "So," she said briskly. "Are we to stay or are we to go?"

I couldn't see Viola's face, but I was looking directly at Winnie. My younger sister's mouth dropped open at the question. Clearly, she hadn't even thought about it. I froze, holding my breath as I waited for the answer. Please, I prayed. I wasn't sure what answer I was praying for.

Mom and Dad gazed at each other, still and silent, for a long moment. I didn't know what they were thinking, but it was clear that they were communicating something without talking. Finally, Dad spoke. "I think it's best that we go," he said slowly. "My sister Joan's in St. John's, and she and your Uncle Charlie have a big house. I'm sure they can help us get set up."

Everyone sat rigidly still for a moment. My lungs began to burn from holding my breath. When I couldn't take it anymore, I took a gulp of air. Like that had been a signal, Winnie and Viola breathed in too.

Then Mom said, "I'm worried about Henry. There are doctors there who can help us if he doesn't get better. And Winnie, child, they can help if your head gets bad again. Here in Taylor's Bay we'll be alone, near enough."

"But live in the city!" exclaimed Uncle Bert. "All those people? I can't imagine."

"Nah," said Eddie. "Give me the sea breeze and the shore any day."

"You're old enough to decide, Eddie," Mom said, very quietly. "But Dad and I are going with the young ones. It's for the best."

I couldn't stand it. Not only leave Taylor's Bay, but leave people behind? Split our family? I shoved the chair back as I stood up, nearly knocking Viola over. Without a word I crammed my feet into a random pair of boots and ran outside. Mom called my name, but I did not turn back. Instead, I ran, too-large boots slipping in the snow. I ran and ran, up the path and around the pond, until I had to stop to catch my breath. The cold wind tugged at my skirt and whipped my hair into my face. Tears sprang to my eyes and trickled down my cheeks leaving frozen trails behind. I hadn't cried over Winnie not waking or about the death of people I knew. Not when I had to face down a bear, nor when I had to help care for Henry. Some of it just felt like a dream. But the thought of leaving, of going away without my brother or Uncle Bert or Nan, was just too much. I sank to the snow-covered ground, not caring that my stockings were getting covered in ice, and sobbed. My nose filled with snot, which I wiped angrily away with one balled fist. My whole body shook. I took gasping breaths that the wind tried to steal away. None of this was fair. Not one bit.

Footsteps crunched on the snow behind me. I turned, ready to yell if someone came to disturb me, but found myself face to face with the large, dark bulk of Boomer. I couldn't yell at him. Instead, I buried my face in his thick fur and sobbed harder. What if I couldn't take him with me? Was there a place for a dog like Boomer in the city? He was used to roaming free on the trails and tracks of our coastline. What would he do in a place packed with people, with houses? I tried to imagine it and couldn't. Surely he would be miserable. But to leave him here was unthinkable. At least as bad as the idea of leaving Eddie and Uncle Bert and Nan.

Eventually, my tears ran dry. I knelt, arms around the solid body of my furry friend. I was shivering, my new dress and stockings damp with snow stirred up by the wind. Boomer whuffed at me, nudging me with his head. His message was clear—time to go inside.

The kitchen was empty when I pushed the door open. Boomer barked once to let me know he was there if I needed him, and I went inside. I splashed some water on my face and rubbed away the salt from my tears. When I was done, I settled on the chair closest to the stove to help get some warmth back into my body.

The door to the sitting room creaked open. My mother's neatly coiffed head appeared in the opening. She smiled, a tired but gentle expression. "All right, Celia?" she said softly.

"I don't want to leave," I said, looking away. I didn't want to start crying again, and looking at her seemed a sure way to do that. "This is home."

"I know, my girl. None of us do. But you must understand…."

"I do understand," I said shortly, "but I don't like it."

Mom chuckled. "Oh, Celia. Strong-minded as always." She crossed the room and sat down on a chair opposite me. "I'll be needing your help, my girl. We'll have a whole new house to settle, and I'm not sure how much our Winnie will be able to do."

I'd already thought of all that. Still, I didn't like hearing it from her. Somehow that made it more real.

"What about Eddie? Nan? Uncle Bert?" I said. "Can't you convince them to come with us?"

"I meant what I said earlier, Celia. They're old enough to choose for themselves."

"We can't split up our family," I said, feeling my eyes prickle again. I bit my lip, hard, to stop myself from crying.

"Oh, my child, it's the way of life. A family must grow and change. We could never stay together forever."

I took an unsteady breath, but it did little to calm the burning in my gut. Looking over at my mother, I could see how hard this decision was for her as well. She looked sad. Tired with worry. There were dark smudges under her eyes and more creases and wrinkles around her mouth than I remembered. There was nothing else for it. I had to find a way to help her and the kids. I was thirteen now, after all, and nearly a woman grown.

"What do we have to do?" I asked, wiping my eyes and straightening my back.

Chapter 15
NEW BEGINNINGS

Sunday, November 24–Tuesday, November 26

The next few days were a blur of activity. Those who were staying started to rebuild, but that happened only at the edge of my awareness. I stayed busy taking care of Henry and helping Mom find and pack what belongings we could take. Two sets of clothes each. A bit of food to feed us on the trip. Whatever small, personal items we still had—Winnie's doll, my hairbrush, a single porcelain plate, its painted birds still bright and cheerful. Most things we'd leave for Nan and the young men to use.

Viola had sent word to Lamaline on one of the relief ships, letting her employers know she would not be able to return. She was planning to come with us to St. John's and find a place there. After all that had happened, she didn't feel right being away from us again. For me, it was some relief to know she was coming too. It didn't take away the sting of the others staying, but it helped.

Winnie seemed excited about the trip. She chattered constantly about the things she hoped to see and about how she wanted to see the world. Automobiles, trains, whales. Electric lights. More telephones. Mom and Viola indulged her, sharing secret smiles over her head. I worried about her in the city. Would people accept her, as they had here? Would they stare, whisper, make a fuss? No one else seemed concerned about it, so I tried to set my own worry aside. Instead, we planned to make a new dress for her doll. Surely Aunt Joan would have some scraps of fabric we could use. Maybe even enough for a whole new doll-sized wardrobe.

We were waiting for the next coastal boat to come by. More relief supplies arriving seemed likely, and we hoped to book passage on the ship to St. John's. Surely they'd take us, for the sake of Henry and his injury. I watched my parents when they talked about it. Mom put on a brave face, but I could see her concern in the slight downturn of her mouth and the lack of sparkle in her eyes. I had my own thoughts about it, and they made my stomach clench. What if there wasn't room for passengers? What if Henry took a turn for the worse before the coastal boat arrived? There was a lot to think about, and it was hard not to let my worries take over.

Ollie peeked in on Henry several times a day, but Gran Taylor shooed him outside every time she saw him. Bessie stayed out of sight, near hiding in the room she shared with Dinah. I wasn't sure if she was avoiding me or just people in general. Dinah, by contrast, flitted about helping us pack and asking questions I had no answers for. Sometimes I wondered if she wanted to say something different but couldn't work out how to say it.

The menfolk who were staying got busy building up houses for themselves and their families. One of the big boats that stopped by helped out by towing buildings in from the bay, where they were put back in place and grounded on new foundations. Eddie and Uncle Bert helped, building a smaller home on Nan's lot for just the three of them. They spoke grandly of the boat they'd work on once things got settled. I wasn't sure where they were getting that boat but decided not to mention it. Why ruin their plans with my doubts?

The one conversation I hadn't brought up again

was the one about Boomer. I couldn't bear the thought of leaving him behind, but whatever would my parents say about bringing him along? He was a working dog, after all, one used to being on a boat. What could he do in the city? He was another mouth to feed, too, and one that could eat a lot. Here in Taylor's Bay, he'd catch himself a fish or eat scraps down at the docks. But shipboard, not on a fishing boat, how were we to feed him? Would he even be welcome aboard? And what about Aunt Joan? Would she allow a great big Newf like him at her house? I had so many questions and I didn't know where to start the conversation.

When I wasn't helping pack, I spent time outside with Boomer, burying my face in his fur. He was always so patient, like he understood what I was feeling. Eddie found us like that late Monday afternoon as the sun began to sink below the far-off edge of the ocean.

"You know," he said, coming to stand next to us and absently stroking Boomer's head, "I doubt Mom and Dad will be able to say no to you if you ask to take him. 'Specially not if you ask the right way."

"Right way?" I echoed, confusion replacing my gloomy thoughts.

"You've gotta argue for him. I'd maybe say you think he'd be miserable without you. Or remind them that he saved your life last week."

A slow grin spread across my face. "Eddie, you're some smart."

My brother shrugged and grinned back at me. "Mom's too worried about everything to see how glum you've been, but I noticed. Figured maybe you could use a little help."

I sprang to my feet and grabbed Eddie in a bear hug. "Thanks."

As I turned to go back inside, he called after me. "Maybe start with Dad."

He had a point, so I stopped and pivoted toward the bay instead. Dad was likely helping with the new house. I picked my way through the snow toward Nan's lot where a skeleton frame of new wood was rising from the wreckage. Dad and Uncle Bert were tidying up the tools as twilight deepened.

"Dad," I said, coming to stand beside him, "can I ask you something?"

He laid the hammer under a bit of canvas to protect it from the weather before giving me his full attention. "What is it, my girl?"

"It's about Boomer," I said, scuffing at the snow with the toe of my boot. "We are going to bring him with us, aren't we? I mean…he's more my dog than any-one's. He'd miss me something terrible."

Dad lifted my chin with cold-roughened fingers,

forcing me to look into his eyes. "And you'd miss him too," he said with a sympathetic smile.

"Of course I would. He saved my life, you know!"

"I haven't forgotten, child. There'll be many a challenge for him in the city if he comes. Do you think you missing that dog is enough reason to put him through all that?"

Tears stung my eyes and my mouth began to quiver. "I can't imagine going without him," I whispered.

He wrapped one arm around my shoulders and pulled me into a rough, lopsided hug. "I can see it, Celia girl. I'll talk to your mother."

I nodded and wiped my eyes with one mittened hand. "Do you think she'll say yes?"

He chuckled softly. "I've no idea, but I'll do my best. You'll have to be responsible for the furry lout, though."

"I can do that," I said, feeling suddenly lighter than I had all day. Surely he'd be able to convince Mom. He'd find a way to work his magic. I couldn't imagine any other outcome.

At last, on Tuesday, eight days after the disaster, the coastal boat *Daisy* pulled into the bay with more supplies. Dad went down to talk to the captain and see about going with them. Mom and I checked our bundles, making sure we had everything we'd planned to take. We needed to be ready to go as soon as we got word. It wouldn't do to hold up the ship. I was restless. Nan sat by the window, calmly knitting. Winnie hummed as she brushed her doll's hair, and Henry was napping. I couldn't stand it. The house felt far too small to contain my energy, so I went outside.

Near the shoreline, the half-built skeleton of Nan's new house stood temporarily abandoned. All the men were down by the water getting ready to unload supplies from the dories. I couldn't see Dad. Had he gone out to the *Daisy*?

Boomer padded to my side, and I rested one hand on his back, fingers curled into his oily fur. He was a steadying presence, patiently watching with me as the boats rowed in and out to the ship and the men unloaded crates and barrels onto the rocky beach. I turned slowly, taking in the familiar sights of my home. It might be the last time I saw it all.

After a while, my father came back in one of the dories. He leaped from the boat to the beach, shaking off questions from the men around him, and came up the path with long strides. He barely paused when he reached me, just long enough to ruffle my hair and say, "Come inside, my girl. We'll talk all together."

I followed him, leaving Boomer at the door. Everyone looked up at us when the door swung open, even Henry rousing and blinking sleepily.

"They'll take us," Dad announced. "They're on the way back now, and they've space enough for a few passengers. We'll be leaving soon as everything's unloaded."

Winnie's face lit up with excitement. "I can't wait to go," she said. "The city sounds so exciting."

Nan set aside her knitting and stood up. "Well then, let's get your things down to the beach," she said firmly. It looked to me like she was trying not to cry, which was a shock. I didn't think I'd ever seen her cry.

"Yes," Mom said. "George, get the lads to come help, will you?"

"I'll take something with me," Dad replied, looking around. Viola pointed him to a bundle that contained everyone's clean clothes. We'd wrapped it all in oiled canvas to help keep the clothes clean and dry. Dad hoisted the large, lumpy bundle onto his shoulder, and I opened the door for him. He winked at me on his way out and I was tempted to say something about Boomer.

"All right, then, get yourselves ready," Mom said, looking around at us kids. "Fully dressed, hair done; anything still not packed is your responsibility."

"Yes, Mom," we chorused.

I was already dressed so I went over to help Henry. He could hobble around a bit, but his leg was still heavily bandaged and sore. He sat up on the bench where he'd been dozing and tugged at his shirt. I smoothed his hair, curly like my own, so it was reasonably neat. Beside him on the floor lay the small wooden boat he'd been amusing himself with. I picked it up. Henry shrugged at me, then took it from my hand and shoved it into his pocket.

"Anything else you're wanting to take?" I asked him.

"Nah," he replied. "I can't think of it at least."

"All right, then. Let's get your coat and shoes on, shall we?"

He shuffled himself forward on the bench so that his feet nearly touched the floor. I fetched his shoes, then sat on the floor to help him get them on and laced up. The shoes were new to us but had clearly been worn by someone else—the leather was scuffed at the toes. I wondered what boy had worn them and how they'd come to be here, on Henry's feet.

Once the shoes were on, I steadied my brother so that he could stand. He balanced carefully on his good leg, one hand against the wall, while I held out his coat. Finally dressed, he sat back down with a thump. I looked around to see what else I could do.

Winnie was up and dressed, her hair smoothed neatly behind her ears. She had a new coat and shoes from the bundles that had arrived Saturday on the *Meigle*, but they were both a bit too big. Her doll poked out of her coat pocket. Her eyes were bright, and she shifted with impatience.

Viola had her coat on too, with a soft blue beanie pulled down over her hair. Mom was surveying the small, tidy pile of crates. I thought she was counting—but why? To make sure everything really was there and ready to go? We'd been over it so many times, I knew it was fine.

When Uncle Bert and Eddie came in, we were all ready. Nan gave each of us a fierce hug. "Be sure to write," she whispered in my ear. "Mail comes with every coastal boat. Don't forget it." I hugged her back, squeezing all my love for her into it.

Ollie and Clancy tumbled in through the door, crowding around us.

"You're going, then?" Ollie said to Henry, sticking his hands in his pockets and looking down at his boots.

"Clearly they are," Bessie said from the stairs. I hadn't seen her until just then. Had she come to say good-bye? It was hard to imagine, unless she was just glad to have us out of her house. Her posture softened, just a bit, as she looked down at us.

"Safe travels," Bessie muttered at last. "And luck to you in the city."

"Thanks," I replied. It wasn't much to go by, but perhaps she was going to miss me after all.

"All right, lads," Mom said briskly, "let's get these crates down to the shore."

"What about me?" Henry whined. "I'm all ready and getting too warm here in my coat."

Mom gave him a long, level look, and Henry ducked his head. "Fine," she said. "Bert, take the lad first. He can sit on a rock or some such while we wait. Eddie, take that big crate there. Girls, bring what you can carry."

We hoisted our meager belongings and headed out the door. Winnie wasn't carrying anything, but it was going to be hard enough for her to walk on the slippery path down to the shore. Viola and I each had a bundle under one arm, and Mom kept her hands free to help where it was needed.

Gran Taylor appeared in the doorway from the kitchen. She looked at each of us, mouth puckered in what might be a smile. "Take care, you lot," she said, wiping her hands on her apron. "We'll help Bea keep an eye on Eddie."

"Thank you, Emily," Mom said, bobbing her head. "I know that'll make things easier for George, knowing there are eyes on the boy."

Nothing else was said, but the Taylor boys and Dinah followed us out of the house. Their cheerful chatter made me feel a bit less nervous about leaving.

Down on the beach, a small group of men stood around an empty dory. Dad grinned at us and gestured to it. "This one's for us," he called out. "Might as well put things here straight away."

We loaded the bundles and crates into the boat. Dad helped Uncle Bert get Henry settled on a bench, then lifted Winnie in beside him. My sister looked around with curiosity and excitement, while Henry looked down at his hands. My own emotions jumped like a fish on the line, skittering between the extremes. I turned to those who were staying behind.

"Will you write, Celia? Tell me all about St. John's, will you?" Dinah said, breathy and excited. She came to stand next to Eddie. I wondered if they'd end up together, and it eased my heart to think that she'd be here for him even if the rest of the family wasn't.

"Maybe...maybe you can call us on the telephone someday," Ollie said, looking anywhere but at Henry.

"Take care of yourself, CeeCee," Uncle Bert said, ruffling my hair. "And take care of the young 'uns too."

Eddie stood back, looking out to sea. "Mom and Dad will need you," he said quietly. "Be a good girl, eh?"

I nodded, blinking back tears. Dad helped me into the boat, then Mom and Viola. The men began to push the dory out into the swell of the bay. Dad helped and then at the last moment swung himself over the gunwales and sat beside my mother. I looked over at him. "What about Boomer?" I asked loudly.

"He's better off here," Mom said. "Surely you can see that, Celia?"

I turned my pleading eyes to my father. He'd promised! Hadn't he managed to convince her?

Dad opened his mouth to reply, but before he could say anything a flash of movement caught my eye. I twisted around to see the large, dark shape of Boomer as he raced across the beach, splashed into the shallows, and scrambled into the dory. The boat tipped and swayed as we all adjusted to the extra weight. A grin spread across my face, and my heart near burst out of my chest. Could it be? Had he heard me and decided for himself, then?

Mom and Dad stared at the dog, then at each other. After a moment's silence, they began to laugh. "I guess he's coming with us," Mom said, looking at me. "We'll find a way, eh George?"

"Quite so," Dad replied, winking at me.

My face felt like it was going to split, my smile was so wide. As the men began to pull on the oars and we moved out into the bay, I raised one hand and waved to the folks onshore. Beside me, Winnie waved so vigorously that she set the boat to rocking. "Good-bye!" we shouted back to our brother. "Keep safe! We'll write, we promise!"

I looked back at the shoreline. The houses might be mostly gone, but the shape of the land remained. I looked and looked until my eyes hurt. I would never forget that view. This bay, this shore, would forever be home, no matter where I landed.

HISTORICAL NOTE

While Celia and her family are fictional characters, the events in the novel were real. The earthquake and the resulting tidal wave (or tsunami, as it is known now) on November 18, 1929 devastated part of Newfoundland's coastline. The village of Taylor's Bay was one of the hardest-hit towns, with only five of seventeen houses surviving the disaster. Hundreds of people along the coast of the Burin Peninsula lost their homes and twenty-five people died. Dorothy Cherry was a real nurse who made her way along the coast, helping where she could. Descriptions of the events in the novel are based on stories told by survivors.

TIDAL WAVE DISASTER   NFLD. NOV. 1929   COPYRIGHT

In 1929, the Burin Peninsula did not have any roads connecting it to the main island of Newfoundland. People traveled by boat along the coast and communicated by telegraph or wireless radio. Unfortunately, the single telegraph line connecting the area to the rest of Newfoundland had been damaged during a storm on the weekend of November 16–17.

After the tsunami, there were not many boats left. The few larger ships that survived did not have working wireless radios. The people of the Burin Peninsula had no way of calling for help and had to wait until someone from outside the area found out what had happened.

When the S.S. *Daisy* finally arrived in the town of Burin on November 21, the captain immediately sent a message to the capital, St. John's, over the wireless radio. The government began organizing emergency relief and sent the S.S. *Meigle* to bring supplies and medical help to the devastated area. Some families began rebuilding their houses and boats, while others, like Celia and her parents, decided to leave and make a fresh start somewhere else.

Today, the village of Taylor's Bay remains, but the population is very small—only ten people reported living there in 2016.

Left: The force of the tidal wave washed houses out to sea. In some long, narrow bays the water level rose up to 27 meters (88 feet).

TIDAL WAVE DISASTER NFLD. NOV 1929   COPYRIGHT

A schooner buried off the
coast of the Burin Peninsula.

The tidal wave destroyed buildings and wharves
all along the coast. People salvaged wood and
other materials as they tried to rebuild.

ACKNOWLEDGMENTS

Thank you to Cara and Earl for always believing in me and being my biggest supporters. Love you!

A big shout-out to my beta readers, critique buddies, and other writer friends for helping me polish the story. Your questions, comments, and suggestions were invaluable.

And finally, thanks to the staff at Second Story Press for their help with making this the best story possible and guiding me through the process of publishing my first book.

ABOUT THE AUTHOR

SUZANNE MEADE is a Canadian author specializing in historical fiction. As a member of the LGBTQ+ community, she is passionate about telling stories that connect with girls, women, and other marginalized communities. In her spare time, she enjoys genealogy, yoga, reading, watching sci-fi, fantasy, and superhero movies, and playing video games. She currently teaches elementary school French and lives with her family and pets in Hamilton.